FEAR
CAME
FIRST

FEAR CAME FIRST

Vera Kelsey

COACHWHIP PUBLICATIONS
Greenville, Ohio

Fear Came First, by Vera Kelsey
© 2023 Coachwhip Publications edition

First published 1945
Audrey Vera Kelsey, 1892-1961
CoachwhipBooks.com

ISBN 1-61646-559-X
ISBN-13 978-1-61646-559-9

1

Monday Afternoon, January 14

Word that music has charms to soothe the savage breast reached the ears of the wartime manager of Seattle's pride—the Grandview Hotel. Harassed by the throngs milling daily about its vast lobby, he accordingly assigned a page to release, hourly on the hour, via radio and amplifier, fifteen minutes of anesthetizing melody.

Thus it was at four o'clock on the fourteenth afternoon of last January that suddenly, above the clatter and chatter, an uninhibited tenor caroled, "I'm in the mood for love."

Every phrase has its own power, but *in the mood* has a peculiar one. He who says, I'm in the mood for love—or a fight or fun or golf or whatever—expects to attain a reasonable facsimile of same. And usually does.

No one ever set to music, "I'm in the mood for murder." No one who says or thinks those words, no matter how deep his anger or despair, sees himself going out to do murder, witness murder, or be murdered. Yet the power of the phrase is the same.

This is not to say that, had the tenor's inclinations remained unheard, Seattle—the entire Pacific coast—would have been spared the headlines and shock of the Madrona Place murders. The old house on the hill across Lake Washington was ripe for tragedy.

It is easy to say that if his song had not found vent in the Grandview lobby that January, afternoon, a young woman never would have risen from her chair, walked straight to a telephone booth and jerked open the door.

Two scarlet spots, round and vivid as Chinese wafers, flamed in Nan's cheeks. She sat very still, eyes fixed on the glass insets in the door of one of the telephone booths lining the lobby's rear wall.

Behind that glass her husband's right arm moved almost as regularly as a slow pendulum, up—down, up—down. Up to a slot at the top of the machine, inserting a nickel. A pause, then down again to the shelf where she visioned a vanishing pile of coins.

Twice he had emerged to renew his supply. Twice, without a glance in her direction, he had returned to the booth to go doggedly on. Inserting nickels, calling numbers, inserting nickels. . . .

She did not need to see, she could feel the effort this was costing him. Every line of his stocky five feet nine sagged from fatigue and strain.

Tears, born partly from her own fatigue, partly from concern for her husband, rose very close to her eyes. Dyke was such a sweet idiot—

She thrust them back, set her lips more firmly, goaded her anger to support her own sagging body. He was also a stubbornly maddening idiot.

At that moment the magnified radio voice confided to her ears, "I'm in the mood for love."

The incongruous irony of the phrase worked like a precipitate on her wrath. "And I'm in the mood for murder," she paraphrased, bitterly.

Topcoat and gloves showered over her chair as she jumped to her feet. Walking straight to the booth, she jerked open the door.

"Don't mind me. Go right ahead. Call every number in the book. But don't expect me to sit here watching you one minute longer. I'm going—"

Dyke's lifted hand silenced her rising voice. "Thank you," he said into the mouthpiece, hung up. Turning, he faced her. "Where?"

His keen brown eyes behind the shield their glasses studied her tense, tired face. Ordinarily her hair-trigger emotions delighted him. But not now, when her anger was accompanied by blue-black shadows under her clear gray eyes.

His sharply defined features grew sharper still with concern. Characteristically he rubbed one hand over his high square forehead.

She was so young, so inexperienced, so dependent on feeling loved and secure. And there was so little he could do for her—here. If she had only remained at home as he had urged her, begged her to do.

"Don't be ridiculous as well as stubborn," she was advising. "Telephoning for two hours! When you know there isn't a room to be had in all Seattle! When you know—"

He didn't hear, repeated, "Where are you going?"

"Where we should have gone, straight from the train. To Fleur, of course."

"But I've told you. Her phone's out of order. And telegrams aren't delivered outside the city. If they can't be telephoned from Seattle offices, they're sent out by mail. She couldn't receive a wire till tomorrow—perhaps not till Wednesday."

Without another word she turned and walked back to her chair. Blindly she picked up her coat, whirled it round her shoulders, fumbled on her gloves.

Dyke spoke beside her. "One minute while I check the bags we won't need, leave word at the desk—"

She stood motionless until his hand dropped from her arm, then started down the long lobby to the entrance. Just as the doorman succeeded in signaling an aged, unheated taxi, Dyke reached her side again. In each hand he carried an overnight bag. Under one arm, the brief case that was as much a part of him as his glasses.

Stiffly she gave directions to the slouched, indifferent driver, stepped into the musty interior to seat herself in the far corner. Dyke followed. Taking the other corner. Leaving an expanse of crackled brown leather between them.

Over the sound of grinding gears, he asked wearily, "Well—what's wrong now?"

"I wish I knew! Why on earth you pick this time to act as if we were committing a—a felony to go out to stay with Fleur—"

"We're not particularly pleased when guests arrive on our doorstep without warning."

"But this is different. Fleur has that huge house— oceans of room. And a gold mine in Huldah. We have a small apartment, and I'm lucky when I can get a woman in for an hour. Besides—we didn't expect to have to descend on her. This is an emergency."

"It's almost exactly four years since we last saw her."

"What of it? She's my best friend. You can't room with a girl more than three years in a college dorm and not know her down to the ground. Why—my friendship with Fleur is one of the things that really matter in my life."

"Four years is a long time to maintain undying friendship across a continent by correspondence."

"But she's your friend, too. What's more, she's your half sister!"

"Not quite. Keep your foot off that pedal."

"For heaven's sake, why?"

"Because I ask it. Isn't that enough?"

After a moment she said slowly, "No, I don't think it is. You can't be ashamed of it! Her grandfather—"

His short laugh was not amused. "Oh, I know all about the great pioneer of these parts."

"You can't believe Fleur—doesn't want it known!"

"I'm not interested in that angle of it."

"Then why?"

He shifted the briefcase irritably. "Lord, Nan, can't you be reasonable? You want to go to Fleur. Well, we're going. *Because she's your best friend.* Let it go at that."

"But it wasn't her fault—yours, either—that neither of you knew you were related until a few years ago?"

"James Wardman Wales was her father. Merely a stepfather to me, and that briefly. Not worth mentioning."

"You certainly made no secret of it those three years Fleur and I were together at Vassar. Why, it was Fleur who introduced us—don't you remember?"

A muscle at the corner of his mouth quivered. "Faintly."

Encouraged, she persisted: "And you were very brotherly, darling, whenever she came down to New York with me for holidays and week ends."

"Purely in the line of business."

"Business!"

"Making you Mrs. Dyke Holliman."

Her resentments and doubts melted like sugar in the sun, flared again. "You mean you didn't really like Fleur! Just used her?"

"Mrs. Holliman," he asked coldly, "will you turn that corkscrew you use for a mind on the question I asked you? My request, rather?"

For a moment she looked blank. "Oh, about not mentioning—"

"Exactly. *Not* mentioning."

"But you haven't said why."

Other muscles bunched at both corners of his mouth.

"Oh, all right," she agreed hastily., "I'll say nothing if that's the way you feel about it. But it's all pretty stuffy if you ask me."

He wasn't asking, her. He wasn't even listening. Chin lost in his upturned cellar, fedora drawn low over his eyes, hands gripped on his brief case, he was already planets removed from her.

2

Monday Evening, January 14

Unvoiced tensions in the tonneau shortly generated a sulfurous silence. It penetrated the glass partition to the shoulders of their driver, rose to his swollen, red, sugar-bowl ears. From time to time he lifted his eyes to the mirror above him.

It showed him an unchanging picture of his motionless fares. A smallish young woman in one corner from out whose pale, taut face, framed in soft copper-toned hair, two eyes looked fixedly at nothing. Behind him, a middle-sized man, ten years or so older, upright as a tomahawk.

Tags on their twin traveling bags beside him told him more. Dyke Holliman, one read. Mrs. Dyke Holliman, said the other. From: New York City. Destination: Grandview Hotel, Seattle.

A slow smile lifted his facial muscles. One hand lifted also to tilt his heavy, flat wool cap a little more to the left. He knew what was eating them all right.

War workers by the tens of thousands and assorted officials, pouring annually into the city from every corner of the country, had certainly played hob with the town. Made it the most expensive place in the United States for a man to live. But they had also put Seattle on the map to stay! These two New Yorkers, for example. Next time,

they'd know better than to think all they had to do was
arrive to find the whole city at their service.

The two behind him were as unaware of him as of the
crowded streets through which they were passing.

Dyke gave no sign of what he thought or felt. But Nan
was sure she sat erect only by courtesy of the tonneau
walls. Every bone and muscle in her body was numb, yet
aching too from the tedium of their transcontinental train
journey in wartime.

A journey whose scheduled seventy hours had stretched
to eighty before the long, overheated, overcrowded train
slid down the western slopes of the Cascade Mountains,
across a narrow, drenched green valley to quiver to a stop,
in King Street Station.

Eighty hours of whistling snows and winds from Alle-
ghenies to Cascades, of fog and rain and clawing cold
from Cascades to Puget Sound. Eighty hours with only the
sketchiest sleep. With only the sketchiest meals, morning
and evening, and those under the gaze of massed eyes at
either end of the dining cars, impatiently following each
mouthful. No baths. No privacy. And—for her—no opportunity to learn why this sudden, unplanned-for trip was
necessary at all.

Their arrival at the Grandview to learn that their wire
for reservations had been useless, that neither the Grandview nor any other hotel in Seattle had any accommo-
dations whatever, had appeared the last straw. But now
Dyke's perverse obstinacy about accepting hospitality under Fleur Wales's roof paled that disappointment.

That her own insistence on accompanying him was solely responsible for their predicament didn't help, either. If
she had remained in New York, as he had wanted her to
do, he would have been spared most of these inconve-
niences, at that moment be assured of a cot at least in the

Grandview. A man alone could have been accommodated. A man plus wife, no.

Or, if Dyke, never the strong, silent type, had voiced one word of criticism or complaint. Instead he had become a monument to endurance, locking himself away in these silences.

Small, uneasy wings began to flutter in her throat. What on earth was the matter with them? Never in her life had she spoken to anyone, much less Dyke, as she had just now. Never in all the years she had known him had he turned on her or anyone in her presence that frozen steely tone. Now to have heard it three thousand miles from home, in a city strange to Dyke, almost as strange to her.

She flung a disdainful glance at the Seattle visible beyond her taxi window. At thick, low-hanging gray clouds behind which the sun had been lost all day. At rootless wisps of fog already drifting about. At street lights blinking through the murk of Third Avenue's narrow canyon though five o'clock was still twenty minutes away.

Trucks, busses, and cars filled every traffic lane. Pedestrians swarmed the sidewalks, clotted along the curbs in chilled huddles, waiting for their busses or share-the-ride cars. Except for the long coat with the thin fur collar, the kerchief-tied heads, women in slacks clutching tin lunch boxes, were hardly distinguishable from the men.

Between them and the dimly lighted shop windows flowed counterstreams of young girls, hair and loose coats flying, shod in wooden Dutch shoes, in Mexican huaraches, in toeless pumps propped on spiky heels, half socks curled about their ankles. Older women, functionally dressed, bent forward from the waist, jutting rearward below in the characteristic posture of long-time residents of the hill-climbing city. In and out among them, impassively ignoring the convention of right and left, moved soldiers, sailors, marines, more war workers, an occasional civilian.

And this was the city she had described so often after that summer spent with Fleur six years ago as the place God made personally! If the day, at least, had been clear. If the sun had been shining and the snow-capped peaks of Cascades and Olympics glittering wonders against bright, blue sky—

Impatiently she leaned forward to peer round the heavy cap and bulging ears. The business district was vanishing behind them. The taxi wound now through a miscellany of wider, crisscrossed streets, lined indiscriminately on both sides with shops, residences, factories. On the left rose the hills of the city, their summits sprouting thin, disordered growths of telephone poles and wires. Lights showed here and there on their darkening slopes. On the right she caught blurred glimpses of the harbor between weather-beaten warehouses.

Not halfway yet!

She sank back, trying to lift her depression of body and spirit with anticipation of the welcome ahead. Trying to recapture the old sense of intimacy with Fleur. True, she hadn't seen her roommate since that January night four years ago when she and Dyke had placed Fleur on a train in Pennsylvania Station bound west. Yet she had continued to feel closer to Fleur than to many friends in New York she saw every day.

Now Dyke's cautioning words had rocked her confidence.

Six years ago Fleur had been a carefree sophomore on vacation in a warless world. The adored heir-apparent of Madrona Place. With Grandfather Wales ruling mightily from the throne. And Huldah, the wise old Norwegian nurse, housekeeper, and general factotum, ruling quietly and still more mightily behind it.

Four years ago Fleur had been a gay and lovely senior, pride of Vassar's amateur dramatics. Then suddenly word had come that her grandfather was ill, needed her. And as suddenly she had given up her degree, her whole future, to step dry-eyed onto that train for Seattle. Those two Fleurs, Nan knew well.

But what of the Fleur who three years ago, on the death of Grandfather Wales, had become owner and mistress of Madrona Place, an entire hill that, rising slowly from the shore line of Lake Washington, rolled to a low crest half a mile inland? All acquired during a lifetime by her grandfather, held through long, lean years for the day when it would become Fleur's.

Fleur must be a very important young woman now. A busy one, too. Her long letters had dwindled to breathless notes.

Remembering Huldah's tall, stern figure, always in the background, Nan smiled to herself. Fleur would be the same old Fleur, carefree and adored. Huldah would still rule Madrona Place and everyone and everything on it.

Fatigue, uneasiness, loneliness lessened as she found herself looking forward to the huge hospitable home and the two women who would soon welcome her back to it.

Again she leaned forward—this time to see ahead the arched entrance to a brilliantly lighted tunnel. Impulsively she turned to her husband, placed a hand on his arm.

"Prepare to be impressed, Dyke. Seattle's famous pontoon-bridge is just beyond this tunnel."

Her hand dropped. She sat back. Dyke's arm, his whole body was tensed—as it was when the law firm of Rensselaer, Struthers, and Bayles, after months of preparation, waited for the judge's gavel to signal the opening of a battle for life—or death—in the New York law courts.

As the car ran out of the tunnel onto the broad approach to the bridge, the driver pricked his ears and watched his mirror for their first surprised and impressed reactions. He heard and saw nothing.

Fog, hiding the lake shores on all sides, might have closed round his fares also. The long, low white arc the bridge laid across the battleship-gray waters of Lake Washington to Mercer Island went unseen. And the highway cutting straight across the island, to a shorter bridge and the mainland. And, on the mainland, the broader highway down which their taxi crawled in now sodden darkness, blurred with fog.

3
Monday Evening, January 14

The jolt all but hurled them to the floor as their driver snagged the car to a stop.

Angrily he turned. "You'd ought to know better, lady. Grabbing my arm like that! If this hadn't of been a level highway, you'd be digging yourselves out of a ditch right now."

Dyke restored his wife to the seat before he asked questions.

"I'm sorry," she stammered. "But I was startled too. I wasn't watching the road—till just now. This is the wrong one."

"You said Madrona Place, didn't you? Well, you're there now. This highway runs through one side of it. And the house is right! up that hill. Think I don't know that old landmark?"

"But those lights ahead, driver. That building. There's nothing like that near Madrona Place."

"Guess you ain't been around for some time, lady. That's Wales Center." Civic pride modified the driver's wrath. "Just opened little over a year ago, and it's already pulling in more shekels than any store in Seattle. Wouldn't mind having a piece of change in that place myself."

Gears ground again and the car crept on.

Both Nan and Dyke sat erect to see the broad, low, brightly lighted building they were approaching. An immense market occupied half of it. A drugstore, dime store, hardware store, and on the corner a gas station shared the rest. About the whole structure spread a wide parking space where cars stood in rows. In and out of their headlights moved shadowy figures.

"Looks like a busy place," Dyke commented. "Where do all those cars come from?"

"Shipyard workers. New people. This country's filling up fast."

"But I don't see a house—"

"Come back after the war and you will. Ten years from now this'll be part of Seattle. Solid. All the way from the lake. Plenty of people packed in all around here now. You can't see 'em because all this land's Madrona Place."

He slowed both the car and his tongue to pass a thick grove of firs on the left, find the entrance to a narrow dirt road that mounted the hill.

"Know how big Seattle's going to be in ten years? A million people! And there ain't any way for them to go but here."

The car skidded. He decided to confine his attention to the road.

Near the crest of the hill the lights picked up an RFD mailbox on the left. He brought the car to another sudden stop.

"See that, lady? Says Madrona Place, don't it?"

Dyke leaned forward, peered out. All he could see on either side was silhouettes of trees through thin fog, fog writhing to thicken in the glare of headlights on the wet road ahead. When he lowered his window for a clearer view, the irregular and melancholy drip of fog or rain came to him, and cold that bit at the very center of his bones.

"Might be darkest Africa," he reported. "Wait here, Nan. I'd better explore."

"No. This is the place. And I see light." Nan's words emerged from chilled hands cupped against the dim window on her side. "The old madrona tree the place is named for is right here beside me. Can't you drive in?"

"No driveway, lady."

Ignoring her protests, the driver turned to Dyke. "That'll be five dollars for the trip from Seattle. Thirty-five cents for out-bound bridge toll. Twenty-five for return. That's the rate, mister, but if I'd known the kind of night I was letting myself in for, you couldn't of got me across that lake for a hundred smackers."

Mollified by the bills Dyke pressed into his hand, he opened the door beside him to lift out their bags. Dyke stepped down, too. One look at the massive, narrow outline of the house looming darkly far back on the upward-sloping lawn, and he thrust his head into the car.

"It's black as a pocket here, Nan. And cold as a tomb. From the looks of the place, I'd say everyone's in bed."

"City feller!" Nan hopped out, hugging her coat about her. "It can't be six o'clock yet. It's dark because Fleur and Huldah are all alone in that big house."

She picked her way over wet grass to a narrow, tiled walk, glistening with moisture. When Dyke didn't follow, she jibed, "You're letting a grisly winter night in the country get you down, darling. That's all."

Dyke peered dubiously houseward. "Something tells me we'd be smart to go back—"

"If you're out here on an important case, my good man, we'll be smarter still to stay." Her voice wore an edge. "Remember, Fleur's grandfather—"

Grinding gears gave the decision to Nan. But as she watched the red taillights of their taxi vanish down the road, felt the dank darkness press round her, assurance oozed.

The driver was right, she saw as Dyke picked up their bags. There was no driveway. Where it had been, this walk now, approached the house on a slant from the left. Evidently Fleur had made changes.

In themselves, neither Wales Center nor a changed walk mattered, of course. But that Fleur had not written about them did. As Nan slithered and slid forward on the tiles, her feeling of strangeness increased, of being a little hurt, too.

Madrona Place was Fleur's now. She could do what she wanted to it without consulting or informing anyone. Just the same it was queer. Not like Fleur.

Or was it?

The bug of uncertainty nipping Nan since those warning words of Dyke's bit deeper. Her feeling for Fleur had remained the same. But what if Fleur's for her—?

Her feet froze fast to the walk. She had a physical sensation of her ears distending to strain in the silence toward some sound. A quiet, dreadful sound, soft and diffused as the fog.

At her heels Dyke had stopped short, also. She could feel the intensity of his listening.

Again the sound came. Weaker this time, fading quickly. They waited, motionless, but it was not repeated.

The two hard-edged bags he carried nudged the backs of her knees. She choked down an unnerved gasp, quavered, "What—what's that?"

Dyke looked from one to the other of the wide-spreading, leafless trees on the lawns before he said, naturally enough, "Might have been someone's last groan, but probably was a foghorn, on that lake we crossed. Onward, woman, or I'll begin to howl like a wolf myself. I'm freezing in this mild and mellow climate you've been publicizing for three thousand miles."

She moved forward, that word howl in her ears. Far from howling, they had spoken in murmurs, almost whispers. It's that kind of a night, she assured herself; then, at thought of warmth and welcome in the house now just ahead, quickened her steps. Before a small, roofed entrance, she halted again. The wide veranda that had circled the house on three sides was gone!

Their bags thudding to the porch floor as Dyke dropped them startled her. She shivered and ran up the steps to stamp numbed feet while she groped for a bell.

Cold wire of a screen door—of a latched screen door— rebuffed and shocked her. This house that had never been locked, day or night, locked now!

Unreasoning anger and disappointment doubled her fingers into a fist to pound on the door.

Abruptly, although they had heard no sound inside the house, a blue dimout lamp gleamed in the porch roof above their heads, It gave to the white pillars, straying wisps of fog, even to their own healthy faces, a cadaverous sheen.

A key ground in a lock, and the house door swung inward.

No light had been turned on inside, but in that eerie blue glow they discerned the blur of a face against the black slab of the half-opened door.

"Fleur!" Nan cried in relief. "Oh, Fleur—it's Nan. And Dyke." An infinitesimal silence, wintry as the night, answered. The face did not move, and they could feel the scrutiny of its unseen eyes. Then a switch clicked, lighting a small, square foyer, new to Nan.

The wide, hospitable passage that had run the width of the house had vanished. And with it the handsome carved blackwood chairs and tables Grandfather Wales had brought back sixty years or more ago from China. In its place was this tiny, formal entrance, a closed door on the right, a curtained archway on the left. Straight ahead a stairway rose between walls to the second floor.

In the foyer stood a short, rounded little woman, re-
garding them with darting, birdlike glances. Two or three
thick sweaters not only made her shoulders rounder still
but gave her ample bosom the contour of a pouter pigeon.
Small, precise round curls circled the small, round head.

"Who is it, please?"

That metallic, genteel chirrup, plus the fact that she
made no gesture toward unlatching the screen, silenced
Nan. Dyke's impatience echoed in his formality.

"Mr. and Mrs. Dyke-Holliman. From New York. We
wish to see—"

"Fleur. Fleur Wales," Nan completed, exasperated.

A plump, well-cared-for hand, tipped with long, crim-
son nails, moved elegantly to unlatch the screen. As they
stepped into the foyer the little woman retreated to the
stairway, mounted the first tread.

Nan looked stonily into the well-massaged face over
which the lacework of fine lines, characteristic of a mind
fed on personal trivia, spread from throat to hair, gathered
in folds below the eyes. Her small nose wrinkled with dis-
taste. The sweetish, cloying scent it had detected in the
foyer unquestionably exuded from those layers of sweaters, even from the little woman's hair!

Dyke, thawing under a breath of warmth from somewhere, smiled politely. "If you will tell Miss Wales, please."

The little woman gave no sign of hearing. Her glance
flitted about them like a persistent, questing mosquito.
Evidently she didn't find the answer to whatever question
she had in mind, for her rouged mouth pursed and her
hands moved to hold back one of the heavy green velour
curtains sealing the archway on the left.

An arctic breath flowed out to reinforce the chill that
had come in with them. Another click and two or three
lights in a ceiling cluster glowed, revealing a long, rectan-
gular living room.

"Won't you go in and sit down?"

Nan would have preferred to open the closed door beside her.

The warmth came from there. And the kitchen lay that way—Huldah's domain once. Heaven alone knew what, now.

But Dyke's hand touched her arm and, bewildered, resentful of this stranger so much at home here, she turned and entered the once familiar room. Her eyes sought the fireplace outjutting in the center of the long, outer wall. Laid with fir logs, but cold! Dyke, a little amused at reception and receptionist, followed.

The curtains closed behind them, but they remained standing, just inside, their bags at their feet, exchanging vocal glances. When faint sounds assured them their messenger was some distance up the stairs, Nan advanced a few steps to gaze about with unbelieving eyes.

Once comfortable, spacious, and old-fashioned, the well-proportioned room now appeared a battlefield on which furniture representing hostile tastes fought for supremacy. Here and there among the couches, divans, chairs, bookcases and tables jigsawed to fit against the walls, a remembered, well-designed piece shone like a good deed in a naughty world of overstuffed atrocities and nineteenth-century black walnut horrors.

Table lamps and floor lamps of all shapes, sizes, styles, and colors were rampant, unattached cords coiled about their standards. Books crowded every bookcase, overflowed every surface not monopolized by vases and trinkets. Almost filling the far end of the room, an ancient grand piano smothered under a Paisley shawl whose fringes dripped redly to the floor.

Her gaze balked, however, at walls buried beneath mirrors and water colors, Currier & Ives prints, passe-partouted photographs, oils in ornate, gilded frames.

Dyke's silence, too, was eloquent. As she turned, he pretended to swoon against a small black walnut table beside the curtains.

But when something icily smooth and hard dug into his palm, he changed his mind. Jerking away, he looked at the long indentation a sharp edge had marked on his hand before investigating what had made it.

A massive, triangular brass wedge, almost a foot long, lay there. Elaborately worked handles protruding from it proclaimed that, within its triangle, desk scissors and paper knife nestled side by side.

His sheepish grin sobered when he met his wife's troubled gaze. "If I'd dreamed—others were here—I'd never have insisted on coming, of course," she began.

As she spoke, the room went dark. In one stride Dyke was beside her, his reassuring hand quelling her impulse to shriek.

In seconds the lights returned. With one accord they swung round to face the curtains. Dull green folds hung straight and motionless. No sound came to them from anywhere in the house.

4

Monday Evening, January 14

A door opening above permitted the wail of a small child to drift down to them. Then the murmur of a quieting voice.

"Fleur!" Nan started for the foyer.

"Wait," Dyke advised. "She—someone's coming."

Someone was descending the stairs. Under slow, careful steps, each tread yielded a resounding creak or squeak. Unconsciously Nan counted them.

As she reached thirteen, the footsteps stopped. The door across the foyer opened, another murmur. Then the door closed and the curtains of their bleak retreat parted.

Fleur stepped into the room.

For a long moment no one moved. This was Fleur, their eyes told them. This was the tall, willowy Fleur of the shining black hair and delicate features they remembered. Recognition almost stopped there.

This Fleur was much older, more mature, more reserved than the friend of four years ago. The clear, almost translucent skin, dulled and pale now, emphasized the size and darkness of her grave and shadowed eyes. So did the simple black dress which apparently she was trying to brighten with a cherry scarf.

Her long fingers in the act of knotting it more securely about her throat gripped the loops as if carved there.

Swiftly incredulity, amazement, recognition—above all, relief—raced across her eyes.

She started to speak; then, as Nan rushed forward, she hurriedly thrust the ends of the scarf into the V of her dress and moved to meet her. The hand she extended and the cheek she lowered for Nan's kiss paralyzed that young woman's emotional greeting.

"Why—Nan," she said with almost formal cordiality. "How nice to see you! And your husband, too, of course."

Unaware apparently of Nan's hurt surprise, she moved on toward Dyke. "Why didn't you tell Mrs. Devens who you were?"

At the first touch of Dyke's chilled fingers, she withdrew her hand. "How dreadful! You must be frozen. What brought you out on such a day? Where have you dropped from? Seattle? Why didn't you let me know you were there?"

As she spoke, she took a match from an outrageous gadget on the mantel, stooped to light the fire.

"Fleur, stop it," Nan protested. "We're not company, you know. Let's talk wherever it's warm. In the kitchen. Huldah—"

Fleur continued expertly to apply her match. "Of course you're company. The first I've had for some time."

Rising, she nodded approval at Dyke, who was drawing a divan and deep chair close to the hearth. "Do sit down. The room will be warm in a moment. And tell me how you are and what brought you West at this time of year."

Before Nan's wide-eyed silence she turned to lift a poker from the rack, thrust unnecessarily at the logs. With a clatter the poker dropped to the tiles. Her hands leaped to catch the loosened ends of her scarf, knot it quickly in place.

"I'll probably get your letter or wire tomorrow," she continued as she left them to draw heavy curtains across each window. "Mails are often delayed these days. So many Seattleites are moving over here to escape the mobs in town, our RFD route must be divided into three in the spring. You won't know Laketon, Nan—"

"I hardly know Madrona Place."

Dyke spoke quickly. "Nan almost had a turn when she saw that huge center near the crossroads. Thought our driver had missed the way."

Fleur closed the curtains over the last window before she answered. "Yes, that's new."

Returning to the fire, she never let her eyes rest on the two overnight bags beside the black walnut table. "Seattle is—"

"Don't mention Seattle!" Nan exclaimed. "Dyke slaved for hours this afternoon to find us a roof there. No luck—until tomorrow night, and then only perhaps. That's why"—her voice wavered, and her eyes appealed to her husband for support—"I tossed him into a taxi and brought him straight to you. We left New York on such short notice—"

Dyke's glance stopped her there. And Fleur's attention, coming back from somewhere, found their bags. "You mean you just arrived today? Without reservations! You poor things. Of course I can put you up—though not too comfortably, I'm afraid."

Again the lights went out. A fir log chose that moment to explode a small pitch pocket with a riflelike report, and leaping flames set weird shadows dancing over ceiling and crowded walls. Nan, in one corner of the divan jumped, then sat still, thankful for the darkness. She knew this veneered courtesy of Fleur's. Had watched with approval at college when Fleur practiced it on inopportune or undesired guests. Now to be the recipient of it herself!

Dyke, his manner as conventional as Fleur's but his eyes alert, remained where he stood, back to the fire.

Undisturbed, Fleur lighted a floor lamp beside the fireplace, walked round the divan to sit down beside Nan. "It's all right, Beulah," she called then. "I'm in here."

A tall, elderly woman, thin to the point of emaciation, appeared in the archway. Her equine face with its determined features was made longer and more determined still by gray hair cut short and, in addition, bound to her head by a net. Hands thrust into the pockets of a worn but once excellently tailored tweed suit, she took a stance on sturdy English oxfords to inspect the newcomers with small, very sharp black eyes.

"So sorry." Her voice was deep, slow. "I didn't—

"Come in," Fleur invited. "These are the friends you've often heard me mention—Mr. and Mrs. Holliman. Nan and Dyke. My aunt, Mrs. Bundy."

Beulah stood her ground. "They've news—"

"They arrived in Seattle today, Beulah. From New York."

Turning to leave as abruptly as she had come, Beulah spied the bags, swung back to look from them to Fleur.

"Nan and Dyke are staying—overnight. We'll have dinner a little late. About seven."

When the curtains closed behind the erect tweed back, Nan, in spite of Fleur's reserve, her husband's restraining shake of the head, burst out, "You never wrote me you had guests, Fleur."

"A temporary condition that crept up on me gradually. *La guerre* is very *c'est* here. Ruby Devens' son joined the Navy, last spring. That left her alone in a big house in Seattle. As houses of any kind are in demand there now, she sold hers and came to—to visit me until she can find a smaller one."

Nan's eyes turned pointedly on a specimen of excessively overstuffed furniture.

Fleur nodded. "Yes. Ruby brought her—a few of her things with her."

"For a visit!" Exasperation and affection mingled in Nan's voice. "When did she come?"

"Last June—or July, sometime."

"This is January."

"I know. She—she's still looking."

"And Beulah—Mrs. Bundy?"

"Poor soul! She worked awfully hard in the last war. Perhaps you remember hearing about Beulah Bundy? No, of course not. Confidentially, neither do I. But she began by driving an ambulance—"

"I know. And before the war ended was in command of thousands of something or other. Why is she here?"

"Beulah?" Again Fleur made a visible effort to bring her attention back. "Well, she's very patriotic. She wants to do something important in this war, too. Her home is in Philadelphia, but she— It was difficult to find just the right thing in the East, so—"

"—she came to you. And brought those nightmares with her!" Nan wrinkled her nose at a whatnot loaded with trinkets tucked into an angle of the fireplace. "And how long has she been here?"

"Not so long. Since—September. No, August." Fleur's reserve was giving way under Nan's downright manner.

"And will you tell me, angel, why you never mentioned either of the—the creatures in your letters?"

"You didn't know them, dear. They're relatives—of Dad's. That is, Beulah. Mrs. Devens is a Wales only by marriage. And—well, every day I expected they'd be— somewhere else."

Once Nan would have laughed at the distinction in tone Fleur employed toward a Wales and a non-Wales. Now her rising irritation overrode her sense of humor.

"And Huldah? Don't tell me she takes a houseful of women lying down!" Nan jumped to her feet. "Where is she? I'm—"

"No, no. I mean, wait." Fleur's hand went out anxiously. "Huldah isn't here."

"Not here! Fleur, if anything's happened to Huldah and you didn't write me—"

"No. She's all right. At least, she was—"

As Nan's lips parted to interrupt again, Dyke leaned forward. "Fleur, when you entered this room we could see something troubled you. And ever since, you've been trying to keep it from troubling us. That won't do—with old friends, you know. Is it Huldah that worries you?"

After a silence Fleur nodded reluctantly. "She went away Saturday morning."

"But where could she go?" Nan demanded. "This is the only home she had."

Fleur's hands tightened over each other in her lap. "We don't know. We don't know."

5

Monday Evening, January 14

As if she could speak more readily to him, Fleur turned to Dyke. "Huldah's a family institution, you see. She came first to Madrona Place as a nurse—when my father was born. Then helped my grandmother until Dad married and took Huldah with him to run his home in Seattle. My mother died when I was born, and my father left the Coast then, went East."

An overtone of bitterness echoed in her soft voice. "Perhaps Nan's told you he blamed me—a baby!—for my mother's death. He never came back. I never saw him—"

She paused, went on in her normal voice: "Huldah brought me back here, was my nurse, mother, and guardian angel until I went East, too, to college. Then she stayed with Granny, and when Granny died five years ago, remained to take care of Grandfather. Altogether she's been in the family more than fifty years."

Obviously Fleur was speaking with her lips only, the major part of her mind engaged elsewhere. Nan listened and wondered for a moment. Then, to suppress her urge to remind Fleur that the man she spoke of as Dad had been Dyke's stepfather, she busied herself with removing her hat, throwing back her coat. But Dyke listened gravely, giving no sign he had heard all this before, from Fleur herself, from his wife.

31

When no one spoke, Fleur went on reluctantly: "Grandfather died a little more than three years ago. And he left instructions that Huldah was to receive a very comfortable monthly income as long as she lived. She went then to live on a small place she'd bought with her own savings. Near Cranford," she added for Nan's benefit.

"You never wrote me that—"

Fleur sighed. "So much happened so quickly after I came back from Vassar, darling. Grandfather's death naturally left me with a lot of responsibilities. I couldn't write about everything. Besides, I thought things would work out."

"About Huldah, you mean?"

"Well, yes. She didn't approve of alterations I had to make in the house when Grandfather died. He hadn't changed a nail, you know, since the day it was built. All I wanted was to modernize it a little. But Huldah didn't even want me to give up the old well!"

"After all, darlings she had confidence in it—after half a century."

"I know. But even to please her, I couldn't go on using oil lamps, that old wood range for cooking, and a wooden tub for baths. So—she left me. And at first she seemed very happy at Cranford. But, living alone, independence, something changed her. She grew hard, suspicious, fearful of so many things. That she'd lose her money. That people were cheating her. That the world and everyone in it was against her—"

"You brought her back here then?" Dyke prompted when Fleur's voice faded into silence.

"Last spring. But, of course, with the house changed and Grandfather gone, Madrona Place couldn't be the same to her. And when—these others—came, she resented them. She made life very difficult—for all of us. Then last week—suddenly—she decided to return to Cranford.

I tried to talk her out of it, thought I had. But Saturday morning when we got up, she was gone."

Nan flung herself back in her corner, threw up her hands. "Fleur, you goose! Worrying yourself and us to death when Huldah's less than four miles away! We'll all go over to see her tonight, shall we?"

Fleur shook her head. "That's why I—we're all so worried. She didn't go to Cranford. We've been there. Every day. And no one's seen her. We—we don't know where she is."

Dyke spoke calmly. "She left Saturday morning? And this is Monday evening. If anything had happened to her, you'd know by this time, Fleur. From all I've heard of Huldah, she can take care of herself. The Viking type, Nan's often called her, independent as a cactus. She's probably followed the crowd into Seattle. At this moment may be tossing a bomber together on the swing shift at Boeing's."

A faint smile hovered for the first time on Fleur's lips. "She did say something a few days ago about going in to see some people. But we didn't pay any attention. She has no friends there."

To Nan, Dyke's suggestion sounded like a logical explanation. She leaned back, relaxing in the warmth circling round her from the fire. The light of the single floor lamp was not sufficient to illumine the entire room. Beyond its range the walls and clashing furniture were unimportant, shadowy masses.

And rain, pelting now against the windows, made their small circle more compact and closer still. She felt her tensions melting in an almost irrepressible desire to sleep.

Fleur and Dyke and herself, she thought dreamily. Three old friends. Already their coming had been good for Fleur. She had more color, had lost much of that strained reserve. And understanding Fleur's concern for Huldah, she understood too that apparently cool welcome.

Far away she heard Fleur say, "Is she really asleep?"

Then Dyke's arms were round her, lifting her, carrying her a few steps, putting her down. Her cheek sank into a soft pillow as a wool afghan fell lightly over her.

She would have protested, but Dyke's hand was on her forehead, brushing back her hair. His voice was saying, "She's completely out, and no wonder. Almost no sleep since Thursday."

That was what Dyke wanted her to be, she knew suddenly and as suddenly was wide awake.

Through her lashes she saw she had been placed on a couch opposite the fire. Dyke, and Fleur now, sat on the divan, their faces lighted flickeringly by the flames. In the stillness their guarded voices came to her, first as a murmur, then more and more clearly.

Fleur's first distinguishable words were so odd Nan wasn't sure she had heard them correctly:

"Dyke, if there were one bit of proof. But there's nothing. Nothing, I tell you. Don't think I haven't looked. Don't think—others haven't either."

Again that bitter note crept into her voice. "This poor old house. It has had no rest."

Silence. Dyke said as oddly, "Is it worth it, Fleur? You don't seem too happy, my dear."

"I'm happy enough. Or would be if—if I could be left alone to do what I want—what Grandfather wanted—"

"You can't do it alone. Nor this way."

"Of course I can. I am doing it."

On that, she rose. "I'll have to leave you for a few minutes— Why, Nan, we thought you were dead to the world."

Nan sat up lazily, tossing back her hair. "I guess I was. Until this moment. Don't go," she urged, rising and moving back to the fire. "Tell us who else is here. Didn't we hear a child?"

Fleur's face cleared. "David? You must see him. It's warm enough in here now, isn't? I'll bring him in."

"But whose child is he?"

"Whose child? Mine, right now, I guess. Huldah adopted him shortly after she went to live at Cranford. Of course, he was just a baby then. Wait till you see him now! I'll just be a minute."

Before Nan could ask another question, she sped away.

Nan looked after her a moment, then, walking to the divan, picked up her hat and coat. "Button up your overcoat, my good man. We're going back to Seattle—to sleep in a park, if necessary."

Dyke seated himself firmly. "Why?"

"Why! Isn't it enough that Fleur has this worry about Huldah on her mind, to say nothing of a houseful—"

"I thought your friendship with Fleur was one of the things that really mattered in your life."

"It is. That's another reason we can't stay. I can't stand it to see her exploited and worried like this. And there isn't anything we can do here. In Seattle we might find Huldah—"

He stretched out a hand and drew her down on the arm of his chair. But when she leaned back against him, she did not receive the consolation she hoped for.

"We're staying, Nan. At least for the night." Dyke's voice was low, so low it barely reached her ears. "Fleur needs you. Perhaps me, too. Perhaps a few marines wouldn't come amiss, either."

"You're right about that. If we stay. If I remain twenty-four hours in this house, I—I'll choke those visiting females with my own hands. They're to blame for Huldah walking out!"

"Then we'll stay. Though you'd better find some surer method of extermination. Choking isn't effective enough here."

"Idiot! Be serious." Nan sat up to look directly into his face. "We can't stay—"

Her own grew still. Only her eyes, darkening slowly with incredulity, changed expression. "Dyke! You are serious! *You meant that!*"

He nodded. "Didn't you see Fleur's throat?"

6

Monday Evening, January 14

"Hello there. You look comfortable. Mind if I join you?"

The casual salutation burst like a bomb over the armchair. Nan slid to the floor. Dyke leaped to his feet.

"Don't move," the young woman strolling into the firelight urged. "You made such a charming picture. Couldn't resist admiring—then walking into it."

Dark eyes like Fleur's but infinitely more sophisticated passed over Nan, lingered on Dyke.

This new member of the household was not so tall as Fleur or Beulah, though she looked to be. Impeccable dark blue slacks and shirt and sleeveless jacket gave her the slim straightness of a young boy.

Oblivious to their hastily repressed consternation, she stepped between them, crossed her long legs, and with a deft, practiced motion, sank to the floor, her back to the fire.

Nan's eyes, shocked still, fixed on the narrow head with its smartly cut, short, straight black hair. Dyke's, on the long, beautifully modeled hands, moving to extract cigarettes from a pocket.

As he stooped to give her a light, the newcomer lifted her face, smiled slowly with her eyes into his. "Ah! Civilization arrives at last."

While she exhaled, her shining gaze moved over his wife. Under it Nan felt every thread, every bone and impulse was being catalogued and analyzed.

"Do sit down, won't you?" their new hostess suggested. "There's a play or book, I believe, about a man who stood his ground so long he became a sycamore tree. God knows there are enough trees around here as it is."

Her voice, vibrant, low, intimate, was exquisite even to Nan's ears. She sank again on the divan, stealing a look at her husband. Amused, openly interested, Dyke remained standing, the better to see and hear what this charming creature would say next.

What gave her that charm, Nan couldn't determine. Taken separately, the woman hadn't a single good feature. Except the Wales eyes, of course. Her skin was dark, almost sallow. Yet somehow features and tilt of that narrow face added up to the romantic, mysterious look most women deplore but would give their eyes to achieve.

Nan resented her even more than she resented the presence of Beulah Bundy and Mrs. Devens. And she was impatient to be alone with Dyke, to learn more about Fleur. Concern for Fleur, bewilderment for the whole confused situation into which she seemed to have plunged, made her feel old and full of years. Yet as that dark gaze traveled over her, she colored, feeling positively dewy and naive.

"You're wondering what I said, if anything, child? Your husband grasped my thought, I'm sure." The figure on the hearth turned to flick ashes into the fire, and the light of the flames revealed her to be older than the late twenties Nan had guessed.

"Do you mind if I devote myself to your husband? I'm afraid I'm not a woman's woman. And what with the war taking everything male, including carrier pigeons, I find I agree with Sherman. That is a novelty at least. One so rarely agrees with anyone these days, do you think?"

The slender, irregular lips curved almost imperceptibly as Nan, baffled, could only retaliate with silence.

"She's very sweet, isn't she? Like a Sara Teasdale poem— simple, clear, and so easily read."

She watched the flush deepen in Nan's cheeks before turning to Dyke. "I think," she told him gravely, "I could have saved that last *a,* don't you? However, blushing becomes her. As Mourning Becomes Electra. Now, why did I bring that up? Doubtless you've observed the phenomenon for yourself, long since."

"I know who you are," Nan announced as if coming out of a trance. "You're Eileen Wales. Fleur's cousin. From South Africa. The artist—"

"Painter, you mean, don't you? In the sense of 'one who paints.'" Her eyes lifted toward the opposite wall, closed as if with pain. "Even the Barnacles refuse to include me among those who art."

Tossing her cigarette into the fire, she rose to her feet in one lithe motion, held out a firm hand. "And you're Nancy Beecher Holliman. You must forgive me, my dear, for taking you on a brief verbal ride. Fleur's undiluted superlatives whenever she speaks of you make me a little ill. With jealousy, perhaps."

Deliberately she charmed a smile from Nan before she turned to Dyke. "I just dropped in for a moment to divert your minds from the horrid sound of gnashing teeth and heaving furniture. Incidentally, to warm my congealed arteries, mental and physical."

As Dyke took her hand, she added, "Besides there are certain things I thought a young husband should know. I think he does. The prospect pleases."

Unexpectedly she turned back to Nan, surprising that young woman in an intent study of her costume and personality.

"But of course I'll tell you the secret, you precious infant. Clothes by Payet, plus sophistication, poise, and chic. Or so they tell me. Personally, I consider it the triumph of material over mind."

She crossed to the curtains then, saying as she went, "Until what, for lack of any word at all, we call dinner."

Nan watched her husband's smile fade as the curtains fell together, waited expectantly for some comment. None came, and his face, as he resumed his chair, became steadily less readable.

She felt as if her own head were whirling, as if every emotion she could experience were whirling too. But characteristically her mind returned to Fleur.

"Dyke, do you mean you actually *saw*—" When a quick gesture warned her off that subject, she tried another. "Do you mind telling me in words of one syllable just what a young husband should know?"

His smile was for her, his words ambiguous. "What a woman!"

"Begin with the sycamore tree."

"Oh, that? She merely meant too many people have taken permanent root here already."

"And urged us to sit down so we wouldn't take root, too! Is that it? Why—this is the first time, so far as I know, Fleur's ever seen her. She's always lived in South Africa—or France."

"That doesn't bother me." He walked over to join her on the divan. "It's this: Assuming all the votes are in now, the unanimous decision—including Fleur's—that the Hollimans are about as welcome here as a Jap invasion isn't flattering."

"I know the score." She tried to be flippant, but her voice gave her away. "What does bother you then?"

"Maybe nothing—about Eileen. Maybe she just barged in on a—"

Nan sat up indignantly. "Simple, clear and easily read, that's me, is it? As you've undoubtedly observed for yourself, said she."

"Take it easy. She was teasing you. It's Fleur I'm thinking about. I deduced from Eileen's parting shot that both furniture and females are being adjusted to accommodate us—overnight."

Nan's eyes grew, stubborn. "We're staying—until we find out about Fleur's throat—and other things. Those barnacles, for example. Barnacles! That's what Eileen calls Beulah and Ruby."

"Listen!"

She strained her ears to catch some sound. "I don't hear anything," she whispered.

"Neither do I. That's what I mean. That's what I've been listening to ever since we walked into this room. Nothing. Yet there are four grown women and a small child in this house to our knowledge. Perhaps more. Shouldn't we hear some sounds of life—feel life in the air? It's too quiet. And these women—they come and go like cats—no sound till they're right beside us—"

"I've been feeling it, too," Nan admitted. "At first I thought our arrival had caused it. But I'm sure it's not that now. And it isn't silence, really, is it? And it isn't peaceful. It's just as if the house were as overstuffed as one of those fantastic chairs—with stillness. Had been for days, perhaps weeks or months—"

"Do go on. What do you. make of it all, Mr. Bones?" Dyke's tone was light, but his eyes were keen on her.

"Maybe it's just because nothing has turned out as I hoped. Huldah gone. Fleur so tired and thin and worried. All these strange women here. Everything so changed. I know Fleur's just about like me, thinks and feels and does things, much as I do. I know Ruby and Beulah—even Eileen—are just ordinary human beings—"

"Stop belittling. Go on."

"Well, I'm scared. No, I'm not. I'm mad. But I've got the craziest feeling they're all scared. Scared to death of something or of one another."

Reassured by his attention, she added thoughtfully, "This house is away off on this hill by itself. Of course, that market's at the crossroads now, but otherwise there isn't a house till you reach the village, half a mile away—"

Dyke's gesture was not needed to silence her this time. Her own eyes saw the curtains move. He sprang to his feet, strode across the room and threw them open.

For an instant he stood motionless, looking down into the foyer. Then, stooping, he lifted a small tousle-headed boy in his arms.

"Mr. David, I presume," he said as he carried the youngster back to the fire.

The child rode happily on Dyke's arm, one hand gripped to Dyke's ear. The other, a tiny bandage about the forefinger, he waved about for display.

"Dawa hawa owz," he informed them proudly. And repeated the information over and over while Dyke seated himself in the big chair and straddled the boy on one knee. "Dawa hawa owz."

Nan fell on her knees beside them to admire boy and bandage. He was adorable, not more than three years old, with fine-textured shell-pink skin and fine fair hair that shone like threads of milkweed in the firelight. Blue eyes studied her gravely in return, smiled when she appeared impressed by his injury.

"Dawa certainly means David," she deduced. "Then hawa means has or have. David has what, precious?"

"Owz." He offered the finger for closer inspection.

"An owz. An ouch!" Dyke deciphered triumphantly. "David has an ouch, Nan. Smart lad. Your painter friend isn't the only master of double talk in this house."

David rewarded him with a smile that revealed tiny white teeth. "Dawa hawa owz. Foo hawa owz. Poo Foo."

Nan laughed. "The Chinese influence on the Pacific coast. Or perhaps Fleur has a Chinese gardener or something."

When she mentioned Fleur, the boy nodded. "Foo," he parroted. "Poo Foo. Bad-bad-bad."

"Foo is Fleur," Dyke said quickly. "So Poo Foo has an ouch, too, David?" He dropped his voice, asked, "Where?"

David's fingers spread wide as his hands rose to the collar of the woolly blue robe over his pajamas.

Dyke watched in silence his attempts to make the fingers join at his neck. Nan sat back on her heels with a gasp. But David, spying Dyke's wrist watch, was now involved in folding himself double to place an ear against it.

"Fleur!" Nan murmured. "You're right, Dyke. Toor Fleur! And David saw—! He—" She leaned forward, repeating, "Bad-bad-bad. Who is bad, David?"

"Careful," Dyke warned.

Too late. David's blue eyes, fixed for an instant on Nan's face, his lips began to quiver. Confidence shattered in his new friends, he opened his mouth in a shriek of rage and fear that brought her to her feet, seeking something to divert him.

Across the foyer, a door opened hastily. Fleur's voice called: "Coming, David. Coming."

She ran into the room, wrapped in a big white apron. David's cries stilled when she lifted him in her arms, but tears continued to roll down each cheek. As she wiped them away with a corner of her apron, the sun came out for him again and he looked about expectantly.

"Oodoo! Dawa wah Oodoo!"

Fleur's hand closed quickly about his bandaged, waving one. "Darling, how did you manage to get in here? Say good night, now."

"Oodoo," David demanded. "Oodoo." While Fleur bore him away, he singsonged the word as if confident he was on his way to his desire.

Dyke strode ahead to open the curtains. "Better let me carry him upstairs, Fleur. He's no light weight, that fellow."

She shook her head. "I'm used to him. And dinner will be ready any minute." She added anxiously, "Don't pay any attention to what he said if you could understand him. He always wants me to have what he has himself."

Dyke watched her ascend two or three steps before he said clearly, "Take off the bandage when he's asleep, Fleur. When he wakes, he'll have forgotten all about it."

He returned to Nan, standing troubled before the fire. "At ease," he murmured. "I'm sure we've reviewed all the troops now."

Her eyes went past him. "That's what you think. Look!"

The curtains were parting once more to admit another feminine member of the household, tall, dark-eyed, dark-haired. Nan's face lighted with recognition and appreciation of the girl in overalls and shirt standing against the dark green background. But the poker face turned on them forebade any greeting.

"Dinner will be ready in ten minutes. And your room's ready now if you wish to go up. It's the first on the left at the head of the stairs."

"Thanks, Peg." Nan moved forward, determined to be cordial. "I didn't know you were here. Come in and meet my husband, won't you?"

"*I* have a right to be here." Turning her back, the girl vanished through the curtains.

7

Monday Evening, January 14

Ten minutes were nine too many for the room with small adjoining bath at the left of the stair well. A locked door in its right-hand wall suggested it was part of a suite that ran across the front of the house.

So recently had it been vacated, it wore the astringent, naked order look of a hotel room. More, it was cold. So cold they could see their breath on the still air.

Though closed windows assured them no moisture had been permitted to enter, heavy rain pounding the panes and their own congealing bones denied it. A tiny electric heater looked as hopeless as they felt about its capacity to remove even the chill after hours of steady labor.

Again Nan caught that scent—sweet, heavy. Not perfume. Wherever she turned it came to her—out of the wallpaper, up from the rugs.

She looked at Dyke in despair. But he, after testing the comfortable, adequately equipped bed, turned to open his brief case, remove a flat toilet kit. Then, whistling to himself, he started for the bathroom. In the door he looked back.

"How about it, hon? Had enough?"

"Enough?"

"Wouldn't a train for New York tomorrow look good to you?"

"But you can't possibly go back so soon."

"No."

"Then I'm staying." She bent hastily over her own bag to extract a wool dressing gown.

Huddled in its folds on the edge of the bed, she creamed her face while she sought to find order among her tumbling thoughts. But longing for their New York apartment overrode them all.

Why not go back? There was no place for her in Seattle. No place for her here, either. Overnight. Fleur had emphasized that word so unmistakably. Unwanted—that's what she was. By her husband! And by her best friend!

Under her moving fingers her chin quivered and she knew a forlorn desire to cry. But tears wouldn't help her. Fleur with all her worries and responsibilities wasn't weeping. Biting her lips to still their trembling, she reached blindly for cleansing tissues she had tossed somewhere on the bed.

Her creamy fingers grasped instead Dyke's brief case. Turning to thrust it away, she caught herself looking down with blank eyes at a folder it contained.

At the corner of a letter, rather, slipping out of a folder that was slipping out of the brief case as her weight on the bed tilted it downward. Her eyes still on the signature, she was able by a bit of judicious jiggling to force the letter a little further into the open. Her conscience would permit her to do no more.

The few words that now lay in view plus that signature were sufficient to give her what Dyke called a turn. ". . . in Seattle, then will I tell you," written in a cramped hand. And below them in larger, firmer letters, "Huldah Swenson."

Huldah Swenson!

She looked again, found in the corner a date. January 8!

Hastily she thrust the folder back into place, snapped the catch and shoved the case beyond temptation.

Huldah had written to Dyke. On January 8! And they had left New York Thursday night, January 10. The letter must have arrived by air mail, special delivery. And he had said nothing to her.

But their hurried departure couldn't be coincidence. Dyke could have received that letter Thursday afternoon.

What could Huldah have to tell Dyke, a man she'd never even seen? What possible information could she have to bring Dyke across a continent in midwinter to answer that letter—in person!

As she moved about, making herself as presentable as a limited wardrobe and the cold allowed, Nan's mind leaped from one conjecture to another. Could Huldah have something to say concerning this relationship between Fleur and Dyke which neither now showed any enthusiasm for revealing?

"If there were one bit of proof." Fleur had said that. This afternoon. Was Dyke trying to establish that relationship? Nonsense! Fleur's father had abandoned Seattle for Boston the moment his too-well-loved wife had been buried. In Boston, eight years later, he had married Mrs. Bruce Holliman. And Dyke, then sixteen, had received for a short time from that silent, eccentric man the affection and companionship the daughter had been denied.

A short time, for two years later, James Wales had died. And in his will, Dyke's mother and Dyke himself first learned of the daughter living with her grandparents on a fruit ranch near Seattle. Dyke had written Fleur, and when she came East to college they had met, become friends. And both then had admitted—not admitted, revealed freely—their common bond in J.W., as they called him.

Yet today neither appeared willing to mention it. And Huldah had written Dyke. And Dyke had come to Madrona Place to see Huldah. No, not to Madrona Place. To Seattle.

Huldah had left Madrona Place Saturday morning, perhaps to see someone or some ones in Seattle. To see Dyke? Or wait for him?

She turned quickly as Dyke emerged from the bathroom, shrugging himself into his coat. But the quick words on her lips died there. He had said nothing to her in New York or on the long journey about Huldah's letter. He was perfectly equipped to do his own thinking. As soon as he learned of Huldah's absence, he must have known where she had gone. Perhaps that was why he had been able to reassure Fleur so confidently!

As she swirled her soft bob before the mirror, she studied his reflection there. He stood at a window, back to her, idly flipping the small silk ring at the end of the curtain cord.

Suddenly she turned and looked at him directly. The arched line of his shoulders, the tight pose of his head told her that Dyke, like everyone else in this austere house, was worried and tense.

Waiting. Waiting for something to happen. . . .

She shivered, not with cold. She was waiting, too!

When they descended for dinner, the dining room was little warmer than the room they had left, though not from lack of heat. A fire crackled in a wide, stone fireplace, toasting the room and a tight row of bricks standing on end before it. From a small sittings room adjoining, a portable oil heater added its contribution.

The chill exuded from the group awaiting their arrival.

Mrs. Devens, an apron atop the three or four sweaters, was placing small plates of green salad mounds about the table. From the unnatural dimensions below her waist, Nan deduced she was fortified also against the cold by several woolen skirts. Nevertheless she somehow managed to convey an effect of phony elegance more pitiful than amusing.

For a moment Nan felt a tingle of sympathy for her. It would be hard enough to live as a non-Wales in this stronghold of the Wales clan. But to be a non-Wales, short and fat as one of her own overstuffed chairs, among these tall, slender, dark-eyed women—!

Mrs. Bundy, filling water glasses with a long though ungraceful reach, underlined the little woman's handicap.

Peggy fiddled with the dial of a radio, producing raucous static.

Back to the fire, idle and stunning in a brief, fur-lined scarlet jacket over slacks and blouse, Eileen was not a harmonizing influence.

No one looked up or spoke.

Fleur's entrance from the kitchen saved the day and dinner. Over the huge soup tureen she carried in both hands, she sent a brief smile toward Dyke and Nan. Then with a quirk of an eyebrow that brought an amused, expectancy to Nan's eyes, she arranged the tureen midway down the table.

"You're on my right, Nan, of course," she said as she moved on to her own chair at the head of the table. "And Dyke on my left. The rest of you can sit where you like tonight."

The self-arrangement placed Mrs. Devens and Beulah Bundy beside Nan. Eileen between Dyke and Peggy, opposite them. A large armed chair at the foot of the table automatically was left for the tall, broad-shouldered young man who entered as if on a cue.

A quiet-mannered pleasant chap of thirty or so, he appeared not at all disturbed by the harem surrounding him. But his smile met Dyke's as he moved round to Nan.

"I'm Thor," he told her. "Thor Satterlund. Fleur's too excited over your arrival to remind you of me."

"Thor!" Nan's hand went out spontaneously. "But you're not the skinny little wretch who made life a torment for Fleur and me six years ago!"

"I guess I still do—for Fleur," he smiled. "And I might add, you're not the superior young minx I remember either. It's good to see you again. Welcome"—his blue glance flicked wickedly toward the table—"to our city."

He left her then to shake hands with Dyke. Nan looked after him in ill-concealed amazement. Six years ago Thor had hardly spoken English. Now he had almost no accent, talked freely. Six years ago he had been a shy, gangling sixteen- or seventeen-year-old youth whom she and Fleur had alternately teased, ridiculed, and avoided. Huldah had imported him the year before from her old home town in Norway to assist Grandfather Wales on Madrona Place. Now, well set up, self-possessed, and mature, he looked and moved like a man of thirty.

He couldn't be. He couldn't be more than twenty-three or -four now. Yet thirty—even more—he appeared as he returned to his chair.

Silence called her attention back to the table. All eyes, she saw then, were fixed on the tureen. Not from hunger! It stood squarely before Eileen's chosen seat. Next to Dyke!

If serving were distasteful to Eileen, she carried it off with aplomb. When she had served everyone but herself, she sat back composedly.

Mrs. Bundy's eyes sharpened on Dyke. "Shall you be here long, Mr. Holliman?"

"I hardly know yet. Until the work I'm here to do is concluded, of course."

"Dyke's a lawyer," Fleur explained hastily. "Here on business for his firm."

Beulah's sparse gray brows rose. "You continue to practice law when our country is in peril," she stated rather than asked. "When every able-bodied man and woman should be in uniform or overalls—"

"So that's what you're doing, Peggy," Nan interjected. "Good for you! Where?"

"She's my helper," Thor smiled. "Not bad, either."

If he had hoped to provoke Peggy out of her silence, he was unsuccessful. The girl's almost perfect features remained as blank as a doll's. "At the Lake Washington Shipyards," he answered for her.

Nan turned to see color—angry color—flickering in Fleur's cheeks, knew it flared in her own also. Mrs. Bundy's brand of zeal probably accounted for the riot in patriotic.

"This soup is really very good, Fleur." Mrs. Devens fluttered nervously into the vacuum. "Really very good. Though I always feel a little onion—just a touch, you know—gives soup more flavor."

Beulah sniffed. "Perhaps we should try onions, Fleur. Might at least help to get the stink of incense out of the house—"

"You Hollimans must have brought this weather from the East, Dyke." Thor came to the rescue again. "Old-timers say we've had nothing like this for more than twenty years."

Peggy, rising abruptly, stopped all conversation. Her head was turned towards a door at one side, listening.

8

Monday Night, January 14

They all heard then the sound of running, stumbling feet on a boardwalk outside. Thor sprang up to throw open the door and permit light from the room to fall across the floor of a wide, screened porch. The others turned in their chairs, eyes fixed on the door.

A moment, later a screen door slammed and a young boy pounded across the porch straight into the room. Panting, blinking a little in the light, he stood wordless. His light, impudent eyes peered round the group to pause on Fleur.

Boots and overalls were splashed with mud. Mud and burrs clung to what had once been a bright plaid mackinaw. His hands were stiff and red with cold, crisscrossed with scratches. A long, red scratch extended across one cheek to his damp, disheveled, almost colorless hair.

The alarm he had roused pleased him. "That woman that works for you," he demanded. "She here now?"

Thor, turning round from closing the door, asked coolly, "Does she still live here, do you mean? Yes. Is she in the house at this moment? No. Take it easy, Jack. Why?"

"Then you gotta come," the boy cried. "She's the one on the woods path."

Shocked silence held the room for a moment. Then chairs pushed back in a babble of exclamations and questions. Dyke rose and moved round beside Thor.

"Take it easy, bud," Thor repeated. "Get your breath and tell us slowly what you came to say."

"I'm telling you. Guess me and my dog found her, didn't we? She must of slipped coming home from the village or bus station. Broke her leg. So she tried to crawl home—up that path in the dark. But she got lost in the broom—"

Over someone's horrified murmur, he raised his voice. "She got lost in that broom patch, couldn't get out. Nobody knew her in Laketon, but somebody remembered about a woman who works here. Gosh, she's an awful sight—"

"What do you mean, no one knew her on the woods path?" Thor was both skeptical and annoyed by the boy's manner. "Where is she now?"

"In back of the drugstore. That's where we—me and some of the men took her. And they want someone from here to come. Right away. Couldn't get you by phone—"

Peggy already stood at Thor's side, her own heavy jacket over her shoulders, his in her hands.

"You go on ahead, Jack," Thor ordered as he pulled his on. "I'll be right behind you—in one minute."

When the reluctant boy had stepped outside, he closed the door before turning to Fleur.

"Sit tight till I get back," he advised, more calmly than he obviously felt. "Jack was so excited he didn't know what he was saying. The woman may not be Huldah. If she is, she may be only slightly hurt. No, you stay here, Peg. Take care of Fleur. Make her eat something. I'll be back or send word by someone as soon as I can."

"Let me go with you," Dyke suggested.

"You'd break your neck on that path a night like this. But I can run it with my eyes shut. And it's twice as far to follow the highway. If it is Huldah and she isn't badly hurt, I'll bring her back in the taxi. You might have her room ready, Peg."

Thor hurried away. In seconds the echoes of his running progress down the boardwalk faded into silence. Silence gripped the room as every ear strained to follow him.

"I wouldn't worry—yet, Fleur," Dyke advised as he returned to his chair. "That kid got a kick out of bursting in here with bad news. Probably built up a tale out of little as he ran. And it may not be Huldah."

His words reassured no one. Least of all, himself. Paralysis seemed to have seized them all. No one spoke, moved to prepare Huldah's room, do anything.

As he looked from one pinched, stricken face to the other, it closed, hiding the tension under which they waited. Certainty that the woman was Huldah lay heavily on the air.

Fleur was the first to find her voice. "Where's Peggy? She must finish her dinner, go to bed—"

Peggy wasn't there. Faint sounds from the boardwalk told where she was and where she was going.

"It can't be Huldah," Nan offered suddenly. "Everyone in Laketon knows her."

Fleur shook her head. "Laketon's no longer just a crossroads center and bus station."

"Huldah never went there, never went anywhere, after she came back here last spring," Beulah added. "And before that she'd lived in Cranford almost three years."

Mrs. Devens rose, grasping blindly at dishes. "I'm sure Thor was right. Fleur—all of us—should eat something."

But her hands shook so that Dyke, compassionate, rose to place a steadying pressure on her arm. The shock or fear he read in her eyes stopped any words on his lips. With surprising lightness, considering her proportions, she moved out of his range.

Beulah, suddenly old and tired, rose stiffly and disappeared into the kitchen behind her. Beside him Eileen sat very still, then too nonchalantly lighted a cigarette.

After a time, first Ruby, then Beulah returned, empty-handed. Eileen crushed out her cigarette, sat motionless, her eyes on a mirror on the wall above Nan's head.

Nan moved her chair round beside Fleur's, took her cold hands in hers, but said nothing. No words of hers, she knew, could drive from Fleur's mind terrible pictures of her old nurse and companion suffering alone in the cold and dark, only a few hundred feet from her home.

Half an hour ticked away on the clock above the mantel. Thirty minutes, eighteen hundred seconds. Each one appeared to add its own apprehension and suspense to the room. And before that half-hour had passed, all had merged in one common fear.

Fear!

Fear of what? Nan wondered, even while she sat shaken and silent, longing for someone to speak, to move. Yet dreading any sound, any movement.

Naturally they might fear Huldah was injured, even dead. But that kind of fear implied anxiety, concern, regret, sympathy *for* someone else.

The emotion rising from this table was not that kind of fear. It was not fear *for* but fear *of* something or someone.

Fear colored each face. Fleur's—a fragile bluish white. Beulah's—gray. Ruby's—putty-colored and dry. Eileen's dark skin showed a saffron tinge. Even Dyke's healthy color had changed, deepened, as if his thoughts were drawing all his blood to his head.

Inevitably both sound, and movement came. In the rattling boards of the walk. In the creak of an opening screen door. In light, fagged footsteps crossing the porch. Peggy opened the door, entered.

For a moment Nan had eyes only for the girl herself. Flushed with running, her hair blown and spangled with moisture, charged with some deep emotion that smoldered in her long, dark eyes, Peggy was startlingly lovely. But she was unaware of it.

Her eyelids raised slowly as she looked down the table to Fleur. Under that gaze Nan felt Fleur's hands beneath hers clasp convulsively.

Then, with a nod, Peggy answered the question in every face.

Before she spoke she took a tired step forward to grasp the back of Thor's chair with one hand, place a flashlight on the table with the other.

"She's dead," she announced in a flat, drugged voice. "Was dead when they found her."

Without another word she walked out of the room.

As abruptly and completely, fear went out of the room, too!

Dyke shattered the silence all seemed afraid to break. "I imagine Thor can be depended on to do whatever is necessary for Huldah. In the meantime Fleur must have some rest."

As he spoke he lifted her from her chair to draw her arm through his. "Lead the way to that other fire," he said to his wife. "Nan!" His voice rose sharply.

She came back with an effort from her study of Eileen's strategic position. Whom or what had she been watching so continuously in the mirror?

Nan sped ahead through the sitting room to open the door to the living room. There she stopped in wonder. The long room was dark, save for the area before the fire, and that was inviting indeed.

Three comfortable chairs had been drawn about the glowing fire. In the soft light of two low lamps a small table held an electric coffee service and small sandwiches. Someone, had thought ahead of Dyke.

He placed Fleur in the central chair. "Now talk, cry, or be silent, as you like."

She leaned back, eyes closed, hands limp in her lap. She appeared very near collapse. Not only from this shock, Nan thought. Only a prolonged period of strain could culminate in that dull pallor and utter exhaustion.

Hastily she poured coffee. "Drink this, darling. Try to think Huldah isn't suffering or troubled any more."

Fleur's eyes opened slowly. "Oh, I should never have brought her back here. That was my great mistake. Then this wouldn't—couldn't—have happened."

"You haven't a reason in the world to blame yourself, angel. For Huldah, above all. Don't think of these past few weeks or months. Think of the years—ever since you were born—when Huldah's whole life was wrapped around yours. Just by existing, you made her happy. She told me that herself."

The cup in Fleur's hand shook so that Dyke took it from her, placed it on the table. She turned to him fearfully.

"I can't think—feel anything. I know I should be feeling badly. For what happened. That Huldah's dead. But I don't. I don't feel anything—about anything."

"No wonder," Nan said hotly, more to Dyke than to Fleur. "Carrying the whole world on her shoulders! Only twenty-eight—and she's positively matriarchal. Well, that's over now. It's time to let others do something for her."

"I'd say bed was the place for you, Fleur," Dyke suggested. "Please go. Nan and I will wait for Thor, do whatever is—"

"No, no." Fleur sat erect. "I'm all right. Really I am. And I couldn't sleep. I must wait for Thor."

She was so upset Dyke said quickly, "All right. Drink that coffee and eat those sandwiches then. And tell us

what's on your mind if you like. You didn't say this afternoon why you brought Huldah back, did you?"

Fleur sipped her coffee, nibbled a sandwich thoughtfully. "No," she told him as if she had come to a decision.
"I didn't. I brought her back—because of David."

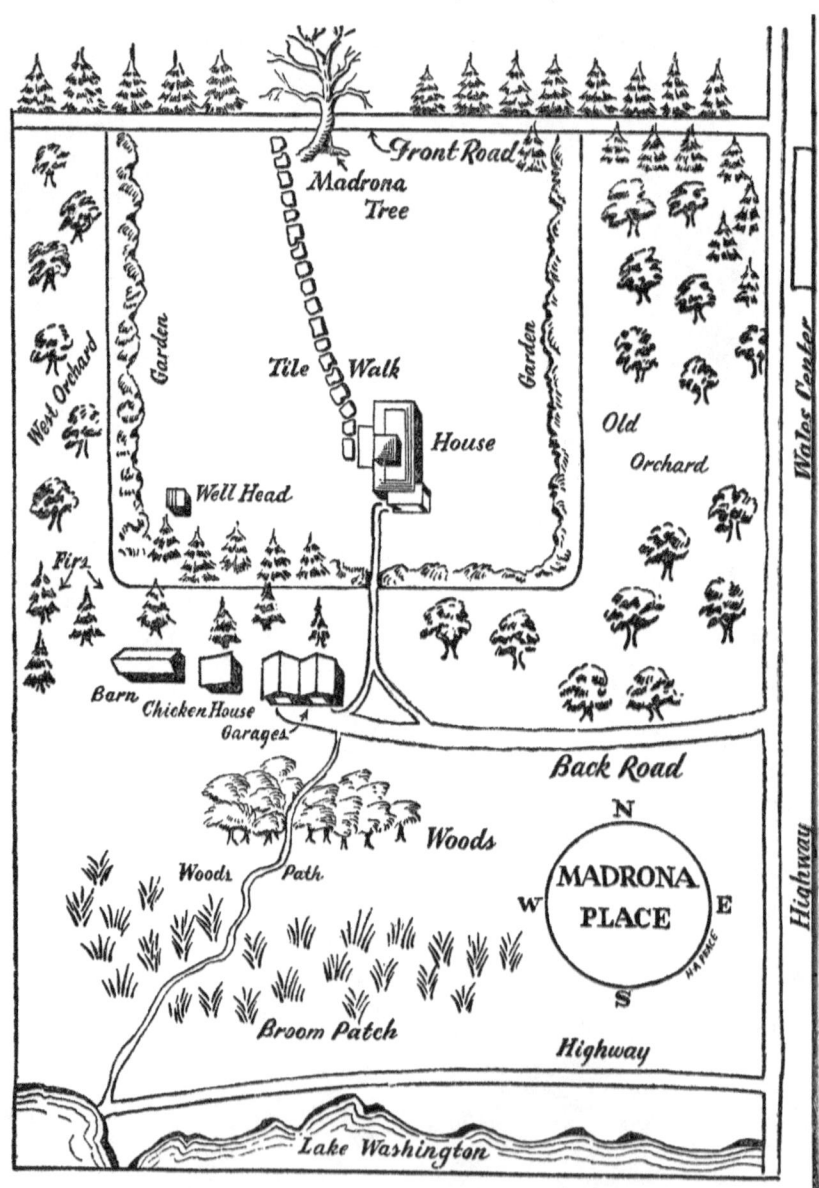

9

Monday Night, January 14

Nan, thinking Fleur's thoughts should be diverted from Huldah, asked again, "Who is he, darling?"

"It's such a long, twisted sort of story. That's why I said so little this afternoon. You see, Huldah found him, adopted him in the first place. Shortly after she moved to Cranford. She'd always taken care of someone. I think she felt lost without anyone dependent on her."

"But where did she find him? Didn't she tell you?"

Fleur shook her head. "At that time Huldah wasn't— still resented me. It took months to get back into her good graces. She told one of her neighbors at Cranford he was a nephew's child. And she has a nephew in Minnesota. But she—she never explained to me."

"Sounds like a good arrangement for both Huldah and David," Dyke commented.

"It was, at first. She gave him the same care she'd given me. But when he began to run about and talk, she was so strict with him, so determined to teach him all the— these wrong notions she believed in herself. She didn't talk much to him, wouldn't let him have the toys I'd take over with fruit and things every few days. Perhaps you noticed yourselves tonight how backward he is for a three-year-old. Though he's learning fast now."

"Perhaps you took her too seriously," Dyke suggested. "A small boy in the country can find plenty of amusement.

"But he was so adorable, so quick to learn. And she punished him so severely for trifles. Finally, I couldn't stand it. I made her come back here and bring David with her."

"Made her!" Nan was incredulous. "*You* made Huldah—!"

"You think I'm soft, and I am," Fleur conceded. "But I can be firm when I have to. And I paid Huldah that income, every month. To—save David, I stopped it. She had to come back."

Nan suppressed an exclamation. Fleur looked up.

"You're thinking, aren't you, I owed more to Huldah than to David? And you're right, of course. But at the time I thought I was doing the best thing for both of them. And at first she seemed content to be back here. More like the old Huldah. Then she began to make trouble with the relatives. Perhaps she was growing senile. Eileen said she was. But I—I suppose I thought of her as the Huldah I'd always known. I didn't realize how rapidly she was changing."

"Something happened?" Dyke prompted.

"Friday night. Rather, early Saturday morning. David sleeps in the old nursery. It can only be entered through my room. Or Thor's. I woke suddenly—certain something was very wrong. It was. When I got my bed lamp on, there was Huldah, almost at my door, David in her arms, wrapped in a blanket. She was going to take him away. She said this house was filled with wicked women and she had to save him."

Not so senile, Nan thought; then, in apology for her thoughts, murmured, "I didn't realize you meant she had— that kind of fancies."

"Somehow I got David away from her and back to his bed. Then I took Huldah back to hers."

Fleur's hand moved toward her throat, dropped. "I thought she'd be all right in the morning. But Saturday morning I overslept. When I got up, she was gone."

"You looked for her then?" Dyke asked.

"When she wasn't in the house, I thought, of course, she'd gone back to Cranford," Fleur confessed unhappily. "We all thought that. Just Friday I'd given her the key to her cottage. And she'd been so determined to go for the past week, I thought it might be a good thing for her to have a day or two alone. Then if she decided she'd be more contented there, I'd send the money every month as usual."

"Keeping David here?"

"Until this bad weather is over, at least." Fleur sighed. "I'm telling this badly. And perhaps being unfair to her. But really I'd been through so much with her, I didn't think about her as much as I should."

"But you went over every day, you said?"

"Thor did. She was very fond of him, naturally. He's the grandson of some old friend of hers in Norway. So Saturday afternoon I sent over food, extra blankets, and other things with him. I thought— Oh, that doesn't matter now."

"It's this horde of women that's worn you down, made you so tired and confused you can't think, dear," Nan declared indignantly. "You don't have to take care of every woman who runs to you because she can't take care of herself. This wouldn't have happened if there'd just been you and Huldah. What's Eileen doing here? And Peggy? Oh, I know they're relatives of some sort, like Beulah and Ruby. But the clan system is out in this country. And Thor and David aren't even relatives."

"Leave Thor out," Fleur protested with unexpected vigor. "He belongs here as much as I do. I don't know what we'd have done without him when Granny died and

Grandfather simply folded up without her. He ran this place, still does, and in addition works at the shipyards."

She stopped, listening, then busied herself with the coffee service.

Slow steps were descending the stairs. A moment later Eileen entered, David asleep in her arms.

"I thought you'd like him down here, Fleur. Your door was open," she explained.

Fleur's face grew whiter still. She sprang to her feet. "It couldn't be," she cried. "I locked it myself." Her hand, searching in the patch pocket of the short jacket she had donned for dinner, came out empty. "I had the key—it's gone!"

"I know you locked it," Eileen told her. "I saw you do it. That's why I brought him down."

She placed the boy on the divan, watched Fleur cover him with an afghan before she turned away. "I placed two bricks to heat for you," she informed the Hollimans as she went. At the curtains she paused to exclaim, "Heavens! I've been thinking of others. The Fleur influence. It will be my undoing."

She stepped back as the curtains opened and Beulah Bundy looked in. "I thought you'd want to know, Fleur," she announced, "that the door of the chicken house was left unlocked again. I locked it. The key's on the kitchen table."

Her eyes moved over the group by the fire, but when Fleur merely nodded, she withdrew. With a shrug, Eileen followed.

As Fleur sank again into her, chair, Mrs. Devens chirruped from the sitting-room door, "I'll take the coffee things— Oh, you're not finished, Fleur. Everything else is ready and everyone's gone. Call me when you want me. I'll be upstairs"—her glance skittered over the Hollimans—"rearranging my things."

"Thank you, Ruby," Fleur murmured. But when the door closed behind the padded shoulders, her lips quivered as if she were about to break into hysterical laughter.

Dyke remained standing, his head turning from door to archway in anticipation of new arrivals. But Nan's quick temper was mounting.

"Is this a madhouse?" she demanded. "Fleur, you can't go on like this another day. No one could."

"It's because I can't get servants." Fleur revived under Nan's wrath. "Every man, woman, and child is working in shipyards, Boeing's, or some other war plant."

"Four healthy women should be able to take care of this house without your lifting a finger," Nan stormed. "Why does this Beulah run to you about locks? And what—"

"Beulah's a bit of a fanatic about locking everything, even the house doors in daytime. And she—she enjoys pointing out small lapses—in others. But she's really very good, takes many responsibilities—"

"And what can you say for little Ruby—Pearl—or whatever her name is? What does she want you to do she can't do herself?"

"Wash the dishes." Before Nan's thunderstruck gaze, Fleur hurried to explain. "She and Beulah can't work together. And she can't do them alone because of her hands."

"What's the matter with them?" Dyke wanted to know.

"Haven't you noticed them? They're her pride—like the long fingernails of the Chinese. They—she won't put them in water. So she's a wiper. Peggy helps sometimes. But she's probably in bed, poor child."

"What about Eileen?"

Fleur threw up her hands. "She's my luxury. I implore her to toil not nor to spin."

Dyke said evenly, "You did that very well, Fleur. If it weren't for one or two things I observed this afternoon, you might have convinced me you were just another victim of relatives and wartime circumstances. No, I'll take that back. One, two, even three of these people under your roof, I'll concede. But here are five able-bodied and -minded adults—and one child—that's right, isn't it?"

His change of tone disturbed Fleur. She barely nodded.

"What is it you know—or have—that they want?"

Nan gasped. But neither her husband nor Fleur was aware of her. Across the coffee table they faced one another steadily.

Fleur took a long moment before confessing, "I was afraid you'd think something like that. I—sometimes I've wondered, too, why they're all here. Maybe not that so much as why—why each one resents the others so terribly. At times when they're bickering over locks or something, I've almost feared they'd harm one another. They wouldn't do that unless there was some deeper reason, would they?"

Something had startled Dyke, excited him, Nan saw. His nose was positively aquiver on the trail of some idea.

"You're sure you've thought of all possible reasons?" he went on, "Property matters, for example? Inheritances—they usually draw relatives around. Secret papers hidden somewhere? Jewels? Other valuables? Or even a personal secret? It's possible you know something without realizing its importance—to others."

Nan leaned forward to look at them more closely. Dyke's face was now unreadable. So was Fleur's. Yet as Fleur shook her head to each suggestion, Nan felt both Fleur and Dyke were talking about something beyond her own wave length.

Except to guard their words, they were giving no thought to her. They were again trying to face each other down. Dyke pressing. Fleur resisting.

Suddenly Fleur cried, "No, no. It can't be any of those things. I don't know."

Dyke leaned back. He had gained some point, but he didn't seem pleased. He looked stunned. Fleur also.

"Then you don't know why someone tried to choke you, Fleur?" His voice was so level and matter-of-fact a moment passed before Fleur grasped his question. She started, moved to rise, sank back. Unexpectedly, she smiled.

"Poo Foo's owz, you mean?" Turning, she looked at the sleeping child, kept her eyes on him as she talked.

"David did that. If you're talking about the bruises on my throat. I was playing with him this afternoon. You know, Nan, making a string of those big colored wooden beads. He adores them. When it was finished I put it around my neck. Somehow he got behind me—pulled it tight and twisted it. Beads interlocked—"

"Then why isn't David asleep right now in his own bed in an unlocked room? He didn't choke you, Fleur, but he must have seen—"

Fleur sprang to her feet, whirled round, almost ran across the room. Nan and Dyke turned quickly, too. But if the curtains had moved, they were motionless when Fleur reached them.

That did not halt her headlong course. She disappeared beyond them, and the door across the foyer opened and closed immediately.

Nan, hurrying after her, stopped as Dyke advised tersely, "She'll let us know if she needs us."

She walked slowly back to face him; "And will you let me know why you looked just now as if something had bowled you over? You were positively glassy-eyed."

"I was. I am. If what I suspect is true—"

He seized her shoulders, drew her close to look directly into her eyes. "And you're to keep out of this, Nan. Is that clear? You're just a guest here—don't be any more than that."

His hands dropped, and he left her to pace the floor as if his idea now rode him with spurs.

"God! If I could make myself believe it's true," he said over and over as she watched him. "But it can't be. It can't *be!*"

10

Monday Night, January 14

That Fleur did not need them they learned shortly when she returned carrying two weighted bags.

"You must be tired," she said, the hostess now, concerned only for the comfort of her guests. "Herewith the bricks Eileen heated for you. I hope they'll help you to sleep well and as late as you like."

Her composure gave no hint of what she had found— if anything—beyond the curtains. Nor of the Fleur who had been so close to collapse shortly before. And her very definite dismissal stifled any inclination on their part to mention Huldah or the arrival of Thor.

"You read our minds, Fleur," Dyke assured her. "We are tired. And if I'm to make a ten o'clock appointment in Seattle tomorrow, I'll have to be on my way about nine, won't I? Nan says I can get a bus."

"Just at the foot of the hill. A few minutes before the hour. Or, from Laketon Station, every half-hour." Fleur's lips quirked a little. "You won't have any trouble. If Mrs. Devens' takes that nine o'clock bus, as usual. Tuesdays and Thursdays are her house-hunting days."

She moved with them to the stairs, giving them what she called her bedtime-don't story.

"Don't raise any shades while your lights are on. Ship-yards and other war plants are all around us, and this area is well patrolled. Don't be alarmed by planes—sometimes we hear them most of the night. Oh, and don't hold back on hot water. There's loads of it, just for you. And don't run to the rescue if you hear lurid noises. When Thor is very tired, he moans and groans heartbreakingly in his sleep. Above all, don't let that odor of incense overwhelm you. I'm sorry, we'll just have to let it die away. Ruby's been using your room as a—a sort of retreat."

She kissed Nan and offered a cheek to Dyke. While they mounted the stairs, she remained at the foot, one hand caressing the polished mahogany of the newel post. When they turned at the top for their room, she was still there, her head bent thoughtfully, her hand still moving rhythmically.

That she wanted to be alone when Thor returned would have been clear even if their eyes had been almost sealed with sleep. That she intended to remain alone was made unmistakably clear when they opened their door on a cozily lighted, moderately warm room.

The bed was neatly opened. Their bags on a bag stand at the foot. Books, new magazines and an evening paper, cigarettes and matches, a night tray with water and milk and sandwiches, arranged on a table beside the bed, anticipated every excuse to descend the stairs.

Dyke whistled softly, then bowed extravagantly to the radiant little heater. "My apologies, old fellow. I didn't think you had it in you."

Nan was in the bathroom verifying the hot water when Dyke spoke beside her. "Come out and look around the room, will you?" Mystified, she followed him but could see nothing unusual. He pointed to his brief case, now lying empty on the bed, folders and papers spread round it.

"I did that," he said. "But look in your bag. Anything missing or changed around?"

After a glance, she reported, "Everything's here, just as I packed it. Have you missed something?"

His eyes were cold behind their glasses. "No. But someone in this house has taken an interest in my brief case. Those folders were out of order."

If the house were stuffed to explosion, with stillness by day, it came unstuffed by night, they learned, when, snug beneath a bank of soft blankets, they blessed the hot bricks at their feet.

Small sharp explosions Dyke identified as cracking nails, a sign the night was growing steadily colder. Creaks and squeaks, a sign the house was growing steadily older. Others—soft, shuffling sounds—he did not need to explain. By the time they began, Nan's fatigue had caught up with her and she was fast asleep.

She woke suddenly as some submerged memory turned like a knife in her mind. Those sounds—those soft, dreadful sounds—she and Dyke had heard as they approached the house! Could they have been, as he had suggested, someone's last groan? Or a last agonized effort to secure help? Could Huldah, returning to Madrona Place via the woods path, have been their source?

For a moment the thought numbed body and mind. The woods path, she remembered, ran over the hill, directly back of the house and down on a westward slant to Laketon. It made a convenient short cut for youngsters going or coming to the consolidated schools in the village and for Madrona Place when someone wanted to catch the bus from Seattle that came in from Cranford and other lake shore centers.

Huldah could have come in on such a bus. No, Huldah hadn't been to Cranford. On Saturday and Sunday, that is. But she might have been there today. Yesterday afternoon, rather. From the quality of the darkness, Nan knew it must be long past midnight.

She shivered and felt for her brick. It was cold, and the room was a black square of cold. She put out a hand to Dyke, sat up with a smothered gasp. He was gone.

As she groped for the lamp cord, movement near her set her heart racing. Then his whisper reassured her. His hand pressed her back on the pillow. "Be still. I'm here."

He left her again. But as her eyes grew accustomed to the darkness, she could see him. Bulky with blankets, he made a formidable silhouette, motionless at the side window.

She remained as quiet as she could, what with shivering for herself and for him. But her mind churned miserably with questions, doubts, suspicions, as memories of the day returned.

As she went over those tense minutes in the living room when Fleur and Dyke faced each other with such strange antagonism, she was alternately reassured and more disturbed. Had there really been someone behind the curtains to rouse Fleur to rush away and Dyke to pace the floor in almost uncontrollable excitement? Or had the cause risen out of that conversation? That horrible conversation, filled with implications, that began with Huldah's death and ended like something out of a bad mystery novel?

She was struggling to find a central clue to all they had said, when again and suddenly she plunged into sleep.

When she woke, dreary gray light filled the room. Dyke was gone. Really gone, clothes, brief case, and all.

Springing out on the icy rug, she stopped in amazement. A busy little clock on the dressing table informed her the time was half past eleven. Convinced it was either frozen or quite mad, she scrambled into robe and slippers and dashed for the door.

As she opened it, the red door at the end of the long hall that ran the length of the house at right angles to the stairs opened, too. Eileen in scarlet flannel slacks and jacket sauntered out.

"Morning, Baby Dumpling," she greeted Nah. "At last someone in our midst knows that noon is the proper hour to rise. Join me for breakfast?"

"It's really noon?"

"Almost. Any reason for those Help! Help! eyes or is it the weather that undoes you? My dear, am I the first to tell you the thermometer is down to twenty-five and falling? Or has your handsome husband returned with parka and huskies to break the awful news?"

She paused at the stair well to survey the shivering Nan from rumpled bob to silken mules. "I loathe people who are bright in the morning, don't you? Myself, most of all. Get some flannels on, my pet, or you'll rue the day. And quickly—or you'll get no breakfast. And that means you'll get nothing, period. In this house no one—except David—eats luncheon."

The impression that Eileen's door had not opened by chance at the moment she opened hers grew on Nan. "Where's Fleur? How is she?"

In answer, Eileen stepped back and with a finger lifted for her inspection a card attached to the knob of the door on the right of the stair well. "Do Not Disturb," it warned in large, black letters.

"Travel is so educational, don't you think?" As she let the card fall, Eileen's eyes went over Nan again. Then, with a wave of her hand, she disappeared down the stairs.

Nap, drew back, closing the door slowly. Inside she leaned against it, shaken with homesickness and dread of the day ahead.

Last night, with Dyke beside her, she had endured those mocking shining eyes, Eileen's double-pronged words. In the end had even imagined Eileen liked her, welcomed her and Dyke as allies against the Barnacles.

Now, in spite of Eileen's friendliness this morning, she was not so sure. She didn't think of those dark eyes as shining but as shiny. And although Eileen's words had seemed simple and direct enough, she suspected each one of a hidden meaning. Dressing, she tried to shake off her apprehension, but she couldn't shake off loneliness and strangeness and bitter disappointment. Dyke was right, she admitted forlornly. She should have remained in New York.

The liquid ice she found flowing from every tap in the bathroom stung both her skin and her pride. Her chin set stubbornly. With her comb she gave a final dashing swirl to her bob and marched downstairs.

11

Tuesday Morning, January 15

In the foyer, Nan opened the closed door, stopped, startled. First, because the large, old-fashioned kitchen she remembered was still there. An immense range on her left
sent waves of heat to meet her, and a warm wave of relief
went over her too at finding this homely room where and
almost as she remembered it.

Second, because perched at ease on a window sill, a
vivid spot against apple-green curtains, Eileen was talking
brightly while Beulah arranged two breakfast trays. At
sight of Nan she broke off to wave her cigarette.

"Come in and choose sides. But think carefully. Our
good will depends on it. Do you or do you not loathe
small green dabs of salad at dinner?"

"Loathe them," Nan voted promptly. "Good morning,
Mrs. Bundy."

"Good morning, Mrs. Holliman."

Deep parentheses about her mouth suggested Beulah
was making an effort to smile. But she was tired, old,
and very troubled this morning. Her voice showed it, too.
"Your husband asked me to tell you he'd come back for you
as soon as he could. By three or three-thirty, he thought."

She hesitated, added almost shyly, "But I hope you'll
both stay here—if you can."

"You see, Beulah?" Eileen interrupted. "Baby Dumpling's on our side. I knew it the moment I saw her. Pick up your tray, child, and we'll leave the kitchen in inspired hands. On Tuesdays and Thursdays Beulah prepares our dinner."

Mystified by all this attention, Nan picked up her tray. With a word of thanks to Beulah, she followed the scarlet figure into the dining room. A sitting room, how. The long table had been reduced and pushed back. Deep chairs circled the roaring log fire.

As Eileen closed the door behind them, she closed also one eye slightly. "I see you know your Beulah."

"But I do loathe dabs—"

"Shhhh! On Tuesdays and Thursdays only. Tomorrow— if you're here tomorrow—I hope—and want your breakfast tray prepared for you, you dote on them. Mondays and Wednesdays Beulah harries Seattle for reasons of her own. And Ruby Devens saves the culinary day."

Skirting the chairs, Eileen sank cross-legged to the rug before the fire, her tray intact. More cautiously Nan followed. Once seated, Eileen said no more. Apparently she ate her fruit, omelet, and popovers by the touch system, for her eyes never left the fire. As her uneasiness grew, Nan found difficulty in swallowing. Why were Eileen and Beulah, so cool, even suspicious, yesterday, practically wooing her now? And why was no word said of Huldah? Almost eighteen hours had passed since Peggy returned from Laketon.

She placed her coffee cup on her tray carefully, anxious not to break that silence herself. Turning, she looked out the broad low window behind her on a bleak and frozen world.

Fog and rain were gone, but frost now lay thickly white on the lawn there and on the wide enclosing border of withered gardens. Just beyond, apple and pear trees in an old orchard that extended down to the firs along the highway were stiff and gnarled etchings against the low gray sky. And thicker, darker gray walls of cloud still hid the east and the snow-capped Cascades she longed to see.

Not a bird was visible, though robins she knew were plentiful here the year round, and blue jays, flickers, juncos, and other small birds, to say nothing of families of quail and pheasant that made Madrona Place their permanent residence. The only sign of life was a dog running swiftly, body low to the ground, across the slope on the other side, of the highway.

Reluctantly her gaze came back to the room and Eileen. Abashed, she looked away, feeling as though she had walked in on a naked stranger. Eileen was deep in some inner world of her own. An ugly world, hard and cruel and ruthless.

The romantic, mysterious personality appeared to have been turned off by a faucet. Even the finely shaped narrow head and resplendent lounge suit did nothing for her now.

As if Nan's intention to slip away had reached her, Eileen lifted her head. She smiled, and magically something of her charm returned.

"Do you believe in predestination, Nan? Or destiny? Or the rule of the stars?"

When Nan looked blank, she laughed softly. "Would you have us believe that your arrival—and Dyke's—at this moment is coincidence?"

"Dyke's here to do some research on a case for his firm," Nan informed her stiffly. "We left New York on very short notice. Expecting to stay at the Grandview—"

"So there is a Santa Claus and Easter Rabbit, and Heaven does protect the working girl! Don't work too hard on youth and innocence, little one."

Anger held Nan speechless. When she did find her voice, she said the first thing that entered her head.

"Why not? To be old and helpless isn't so good around here, is it?"

Eileen astounded her by nodding approval. "That's better. Blotting-paper minds! God!" She threw away one cigarette, lighted another.

Nan took time to identify the owners of the blotting-paper minds.

"Now, let's talk," Eileen said calmly. "But not about Huldah. She was hardly a helpless old woman, my dear. And she's now where she deserves to be—I hope."

She smiled into Nan's stony face. "Don't freeze up on me after showing encouraging signs of life. What are you thinking?"

"I'm thinking of Fleur. Upstairs alone. And about that sign on her door. An hour ago I couldn't understand it. I do now." Nan's voice was stony, too, her meaning unmistakable.

"People, people all around and not a tear to shed?" Eileen suggested. "I'm afraid you're right. Tears are a luxury. I can't afford them. Neither can Beulah nor Ruby. Peggy, too, for that matter."

Her eyes measured Nan again. "I was young once, believe it or not. A little girl, growing up in Capetown. Sounds interesting, doesn't it, different? It wasn't. My father was an importer. A very good importer. But we had only a very modest home, lived very simply. Why? Because every copper my father could save, he invested in land."

Dimly Nan resented her manner, her tone, and her choice of words. Eileen seemed bent on giving a cynical imitation of a placid nurse, telling simple tales to a child.

"He used to tell me about Grandfather Wales—and Madrona Place," Eileen continued, adding pathos to her voice now. "But there was never any money to send me to the States to visit my wonderful grandfather. Why? Because even the few hundred dollars that would have cost him would one day mean more to him—invested in land."

"That was Grandfather Wales' chief ambition, too," Nan said, softening. "To own land."

"My father was his son. As was Fleur's. He is dead now, and so is my mother. Fortunately they died without learning the land they'd sacrificed so much for had little value."

Eileen slanted a liquid glance at Nan, went on. "By sheer will power when I was seventeen I won an art fellowship to study for three years in Paris. And I lived in France from then on until—the Nazis came. Escaping to England, I lost everything."

She paused, for emphasis. "So, all my tears are shed."

Nan was silent. There was nothing to say, really. The mockery underlying Eileen's primer-like words asked for no sympathy.

"Shall I tell you another story? About Beulah? My father's sister. Her husband—an Englishman—was killed in the first World War. She drove an ambulance, did other things, until the war ended. Then she came back to this country. She didn't have a lot of money, but enough to insure a comfortable income for the rest of her life. But she is a Wales. Invested most of it in land. . . .

"And what about Ruby? She married a Wales, poor fool. A cousin of my father's. Paul Devens, put everything he saved also into land. When he died fifteen years ago, the land was valueless. On a small insurance Ruby clung to their home, reared their one son. Ruby has illusions of grandeur about the Wales name. She wouldn't dim its bright splendor—neither would Beulah—by working. . ."

Uncomfortably Nan stirred. Eileen's simple words were sharply double-pronged, she knew. Saying one thing for her ears, while they jabbed suspicion awake in her mind. She didn't want to hear these personal stories; yet, since

Eileen had said so much, she might as well learn more. More about another Wales. James Wardman Wales.

But Eileen did not mention him, perhaps believing that Dyke must have told her about his stepfather. To ask Eileen now would be to reveal that he hadn't, would also be disloyal to Dyke. Nan bit that question back, asked instead, "And Peggy?"

"Peg could find a few tears perhaps. But her mother—Frances Wales—wouldn't. And Fran has no reverence for the sacred Wales name. She couldn't prevent her husband from indulging in the family vice. But she could work herself. That's what she's doing now. Personnel manager for some airplane company in the East. Peg's father was drowned three years ago while fishing somewhere in Canada. She's never had reason to realize it's Fran who earns the money that makes life so pleasant for her."

"I knew Fran had always earned a good income," Nan admitted. "She and my mother are old friends."

Aware that that wasn't the comment Eileen wanted from her, she managed finally, "Desire to own land seems as definitely a Wales trait as height and dark eyes."

That wasn't what Eileen wanted either. "Yes, go on. You're thinking something else."

"Just wondering a little," Nan confessed. "It won't sound well in words, I'm afraid. I was thinking it's too bad your father—and the others—hadn't had the opportunity or foresight or whatever it was that made Grandfather Wales such a genius about land. I know, of course, from what he told me six years ago and from things Fleur's said, he didn't have an easy time for years and years holding onto all this land Fleur owns now. But he did. And now all he believed about its value is coming true."

"It is, isn't it?" said Eileen.

Mockery was back in her voice, in her eyes, too. And yet—though Nan could scarcely credit it—her innocuous, heavy-footed words seemed to have startled Eileen. Astonished her, at least.

She leaned forward, her eyes probing Nan's. Leaned back. "Don't tell me I've pulled out all the stops for the wrong Holliman!"

12

Tuesday Noon, January 15

Before Nan could recover from her own astonishment, a deep voice called, "Mrs. Holliman! Nan!"

She looked up to meet the sharp, peremptory gaze of Beulah Bundy. How long she had been standing in the partly opened door, Nan couldn't guess, but from her expression it was plain she had heard at least some words.

"Fleur wants you. Upstairs. Right away—if you're finished."

With relief Nan picked up her tray, avoiding Eileen's watching eyes. Mrs. Bundy said no more until they were in the kitchen and the door closed. Then, unexpectedly, she smiled.

"Fleur's in no hurry, I guess. I just looked in to see if you'd like more coffee. Thought you weren't enjoying yourself too much, so—tried to help you out."

Stooping, she added in what for her was a whisper, "Best guard your tongue when you're talking with that one. She's capable of making four out of one and one any day. Same way she makes things to scare you out of a year's growth from an innocent tree."

"Tree?"

"Wait till you see some of her paintings. 'Studies,' she calls 'em." Mrs. Bundy tossed that theme overboard. "Fleur say any more to you about Huldah?"

Nan shook her head, edged toward the foyer door.

"Nor to me. To any of us. Except Thor, last night, I guess. She's taking it pretty hard, shut away up there by herself."

Her eyes bored into Nan's. "You spent a whole summer here with Fleur while Grandfather Wales was still alive, didn't you? Must have seen a lot of Huldah. She was pretty close to him, wasn't she? Knew the ins and outs of all his affairs, didn't she? Helped him with other things—than letters?"

Nan backed away, took refuge in ignorance. "I don't know. Really, I don't, Mrs. Bundy. When I visited Fleur, Huldah was awfully busy. Fleur's grandmother was an invalid then, in bed all the time. Huldah took care of her. Of all of us, as if we were babies. And she was canning, too. Tons of—"

"I just wondered." Frost tipped Mrs. Bundy's gaze. "To hear Fleur talk, Huldah knew all, saw all, did everything. Personally I thought her a nosy old busybody. Much better off dead."

She was still talking when Nan reached the foyer, closed the door gratefully behind her, and fled up the stairs.

The "Do Not Disturb" sign was still hanging from the knob when she rapped on Fleur's door. After a moment it opened and Fleur, annoyance plain, looked out. At sight of Nan she flung it wide and with a quick hand drew her in.

"Darling, it's like you to come. If you only knew how much I've wanted you." She hurried to plump up the cushions in a low chair before the fire. "Sit here. While I say I—I've been too ashamed to face you. Or Dyke. He's tearing Seattle apart this minute, I'm afraid, to find a place to take you—away from this house. Isn't he?"

Nan watched her with concern. Fleur's eyes were feverishly bright and anxious in a bluish-white face. Her voice brittle.

With all her heart Nan hoped Fleur was right. She said evasively, "I don't know. And won't know till this afternoon when he comes back. He can't phone—"

"That wretched phone! It's always out of order. But, Nan, don't let him take you away. I want you—both of you—to stay here as long as you can. I've thought of a dozen ways to make you more comfortable. Forgive me, darling, and make him forgive me too for being so stiff and inhospitable yesterday. Say you'll stay—"

"But you have too many people here now, dear."

Fleur's anxious eyes grew more anxious still. "I was afraid you'd feel that way. And I can't do anything about it immediately. Especially not in this weather. But if you'll stay, I'll keep them out of your hair. Out of your sight, most of the time. Ruby will surely find something soon. And Beulah is more discouraged every time she comes back from Seattle. They may both leave any day now."

"But Eileen. Peggy, too. And—"

"I can't do anything about Eileen, Nan. Her home's in Capetown, and there's no possible way for her to get back to it now. Peggy—well, her mother thought she'd be safer here with me, working in a war plant in the country, than in some big industrial city in the East. You see, she left college last spring determined to do war work. And she's only twenty."

Nan listened with but half her mind. The other half was concerned with Huldah. But Fleur gave her no opportunity to ask questions.

"Neither Eileen nor Peggy is impossible, really, Nan. It's just that they both loathe Beulah and Ruby. And for some reason I can't fathom—one another. But neither of them matters, dear. Peg leaves the house with Thor before seven every morning, doesn't return until almost five. Usually she's so tired, she goes right to bed after dinner.

Eileen is out of the house, all day, painting and sketching. It's this dreadful cold that keeps her indoors now."

Fleur drew her chair closer, to place a hand on Nan's arm. "It's hard for you to understand my household, I know. You with a modern apartment in New York. And a husband like Dyke. Darling, he's really fine, isn't he? Thor likes him too, wants him to stay."

Before Nan could speak, she went on, "Tell me something about Dyke. Not because I'm curious. It's wonderful for you if he doesn't have to enter the service. But if I could assure Beulah he has an exemption—"

Nan swallowed hard. "He hasn't made anything yet—because of his eyes. But he keeps trying. We—don't talk about it—much."

"We won't now, then. Though I did ask partly for myself. I—I thought if he did have to go, Nan, perhaps you'd stay here with me till he comes back."

"Fleur, you idiot!" Nan threw up her hands, half laughing, half crying. "Then you'd have another Auntie Doleful on your neck. And wouldn't that be dandy? You brooding over David, Peggy over Thor, and— What's the matter?"

"Nothing, really. Perhaps I was surprised because you suspected Peggy—I shouldn't have been, should I? I remember, now, you were always scenting romance—in unlikely places."

When Nan was silent, Fleur said hurriedly, "I wasn't being catty, dear. Just matriarchal, as you called me last night. Peg's mother would turn a handspring if she could have heard you. And don't cultivate that idea. There's nothing in it, I'm sure."

"What if there were? Thor's all right. I like him a lot. A lot better than I do the chilblain she's grown up to be."

"Thor's grand. It's not that. But Peg's susceptible. That's one reason Fran sent her to me. She doesn't want the child to think of marriage until she finishes college."

She rose to move beyond Nan to a door on the far side of the fireplace. "Let's forget them all, shall we? You recognize this room, of course. It used to be the grandparents'. And the next one, the old nursery, is still just that. Come and see."

She opened the door, a finger at her lips, stepped back for Nan to enter.

On a soft white rug before the screened fire in the long, gaily decorated room, David lay asleep. Around him a collection of stuffed animals, dolls, blocks, and trains had been tossed aside. In his arms, his face buried in it, was an old gray sweater.

"What's that?" Nan whispered.

"His—his Oodoo. He loves it, more than any toy."

Nan's throat tightened as she looked at the sleeping child. From the shine on his cheeks, the way his arms clung to the worn sweater, he obviously had cried himself to sleep.

Fleur stooped, picked him up, sweater and all, and cradling him in her arms, carried him to the small white bed against the wall.

As she bent over him, tucking in a soft white blanket, Nan's throat tightened still more. Fleur's face—every line of her body tender for David. Fleur, adoring some other woman's child!

13

Tuesday Noon, January 15

"Darling, I've got to say something and you must listen," Nan began the moment they returned to Fleur's room. "You're making a mistake to let yourself be loaded down with all these women who mean nothing to you. But that's not fatal. You can get rid of them whenever you wish. But you can't do that with David, Fleur."

"David!" Fleur, stooping to shake coals on her fire, let them spill to the tiles as she turned to rise.

"Wait. He's adorable, I know. And you adore him. But he isn't your child, darling. You don't even know who he is—whether his parents are living or dead. And you're growing much too fond of him. It will break his heart—yours, too—one day—"

"Sit down, Nan, please."

Nan knew something of Fleur's firmness then. She sat down. Fleur stood in front of her, spoke with finality.

"I know you don't approve of David being here. But he is. And I've already grown too fond of him, as you put it. I'll never let him go. I'm going to adopt him."

"Fleur, you're not! You mustn't." Aghast, Nan rose too, to face her. "One day, soon, perhaps, you'll marry. Have children of your own."

She stopped, watching Fleur change before her eyes. The bluish tinge had left her face. Faint color smoothed

over it. Fleur's eyes were losing their tight control, softening, shimmering with tears. When she spoke a tremor
quivered in her soft voice.

"My mind is made up—for several reasons, Nan." She
moved to her chair, to find the handkerchief tucked down
inside the cushion. Reluctantly Nan sat down too.

"Name one," she challenged.

"All right. One is that after this war a great many
women—like me—aren't going to have husbands."

"Rub that idea out, as far as you're concerned. What
are the others?"

"Well, another is that this houseful of women isn't as
odd as you and Dyke think. In New York, perhaps, you
wouldn't notice what's happening. Here, where I know
every house for miles around and everyone in them, I can
already see one effect of this war. It's breaking up families—that's true. Taking men and women into the services
and war industries. But in another way it's bringing families together—women of the families, that is. . . . Daugh-
ters who have lost their husbands, returning home with
or without children. Or granddaughters coming back.
Or aunts, sisters, cousins, nieces. Even women—just old
friends—are coming together under one roof. And sometimes not such old friends—or close relatives. As here—in
my home. In house after house around here, you'll find
two, three, even more, women where there was just one
before the war."

"What's that got to do with David?"

"This. I inherited more than land and money from
Grandfather Wales. He was a real patriarch—with a sense
of responsibility for his family. I'll always have a place
here for any Wales who need a home."

"David is not a Wales."

"Wait. I'm not as noble as I sound. I've thought of
myself, too. I'm willing to have people—like Beulah and

Ruby. But I want someone of my own. Someone who belongs to me. Someone who loves me and that I can love.
Someone young and, growing—to keep me alive and free—
from becoming petty and jealous and, oh—free from the
smothering humdrum of living with people who don't really care for me, for anything but security for themselves.
That's what David does for me."

"Darling! You make all this sound so plausible, even
appealing. I feel like a brute, not to be more sympathetic.
But I'll only concerned about one woman. That's you,
dear. And I won't let you lead me away from the point.
You're just asking for trouble if you adopt David. Please
think it over, darling. Wait. Talk—talk to Dyke."

"I have thought it over—for months and months. And—
it is too late. I'm not going to adopt David, Nan. I—have
adopted him. I just haven't told anyone yet."

Nan sealed her lips then, crushing back further protests, discarding questions, comments. "Then the sooner
everyone knows, the better," she said finally.

"I want to tell them. That's why I want you—and
Dyke—to stay. I mean, that's one reason." Fleur's hand
closed on Nan's. "You're my closest friend, darling. I never
understood until I came back from college just how—how
close you were to me. It wasn't easy to adjust to the idea
we'd never be together again."

"I know. Vassar—New York—weren't the same to me
either—because you weren't there, Fleur."

"We don't need to talk about that. I spoke of it now
because—in spite of the way I acted yesterday, you must
have known—"

"I knew, and Dyke knew that even if you didn't want us
here, you needed us, Fleur. And now here I am. Out with
whatever's on your mind."

"David. I'm afraid—for him—if I tell. I'm afraid the
others will resent him."

"So what! This is your home, your life. Live it as you want to live it."

"It's not as easy as that."

"Why isn't it? You left Vassar, in the middle of your senior year, to come back here to your Grandfather. Did any of these women lift a finger to help him then? And, did he leave a penny to them? He left every single thing—property, money, home, everything—to you."

Nan paused to smile encouragement. "Cheer up, angel. You're an independent woman now. You don't have to ask or take advice from anyone, even me."

Fleur was not encouraged. "That's what—worries me. Now I have David, I must provide for him in case anything should happen to me. And they—all of them, except Thor, of course—would receive less. Because of David."

Impatiently Nan jumped to her feet. "Honestly, Fleur, you do get me down. Here you are, twenty-eight and need-ing only rest and peace of mind, I'd say, to be physically perfect. Yet you talk and act as if you were a thousand. It's the poisoned air these suspicious, jealous, morbid old—and young—harpies generate around you. Get rid of them. Now. Today. This minute. Keep David. And live happily ever after."

Fleur shook her head. "Now you're leading me away from the point. And the point is—with you and Dyke here, I'd feel safe."

"Safe!"

"No, no. I mean, I'd feel better about telling them David is now a permanent member of my family. With you here, to help me watch over him until they accept the idea, my heart wouldn't be in my mouth—"

"What are you saying?" Nan gazed at her incredulously. "That David or you or both of you are in danger—in your own home!"

Behind her eyes her wits were racing. She longed for Dyke and the assurance he could give them of a sane and stable world. Even a world with the most terrible of all wars in it seemed more understandable than this warm, charming room where Fleur locked herself away alone to look across a void of suspicion and fear.

She shook her head as if to shake off delusion. But Fleur was still there, looking at her with that sick dread in her too-bright eyes.

Nan's own eyes flew to Fleur's throat, Wrapped closely now in a black-and-white ascot. Uneasily she glanced toward the door before leaning forward to whisper, "Fleur, those marks on your throat— Do—does someone already suspect—know—about David? Has someone tried—"

Fleur's face closed like a white door for a moment. Then she threw herself forward to bury her head on Nan's shoulder.

"I don't know. I don't know. I just know I'm a prisoner in my own home. And I'm afraid—so terribly frightened."

But when Nan's arms closed about her, Fleur abruptly released herself, sat back in her chair, dabbing at her eyes with her handkerchief.

"Do you know what we've been doing, Nan? Simply reveling in a good old collegiate emotional orgy! I suppose we were both ripe for it. You're tired out after that long trip. But I have no excuse really. Except a rush of self-pity to the I head. Seeing you, so young and pretty and free, facing such a happy future while I—"

She tossed the handkerchief away angrily. "I thought it was going to be so wonderful to have this beautiful old place for my own. To live here and to carry out all the things Grandfather Wales had planned. But what have I had? Just trouble and trouble with a houseful of women I hardly know."

Baffled by Fleur's swift changes from one extreme to the other, angry too, Nan sat back in her own chair.

"There I go again," Fleur told her. "You see, that's all it is. Self-pity! It fills my mind with forebodings that haven't a toe hold in fact."

Nan leaped on the opening she had been waiting for. "Wouldn't you call Huldah a—fact, Fleur?"

14

Tuesday Afternoon, January 15

Again Fleur changed before her eyes, returning to the tightly controlled, feverish-eyed young woman who had opened the door to her.

"Don't—don't talk about Huldah, Nan."

"I know, dear. We won't talk about her as—Huldah. But there must be arrangements to be made, all sorts of things to be done, that Dyke or I could do for you."

"I—we don't know what to do yet. She was taken in to Seattle."

"Seattle! Why?"

"Because that awful boy ran all the way to the drugstore when he found her instead of coming here. Oh, he can't be blamed for that, I suppose. Thor's warned him off the hill many times for stealing fruit. He may have been afraid to come. But the result was that the druggist phoned the county coroner, thinking her a stranger. The ambulance was there when Thor arrived. He's in Seattle now, I suppose. He had to go back again this morning."

Nan moistened her lips. "I didn't tell you—I didn't realize myself till hours later. Fleur, as Dyke and I came up the walk last night we heard the—the strangest sound. Like a moan or groan. Dyke finally decided it was a fog-horn on the lake. But it might have been Huldah. If we'd only looked, told someone— We might have reached her—in time."

Fleur's face was pinched with horror. "Heard her! Heard Huldah!"

"We heard some really desperate sound, twice." Nan shivered. "I keep thinking about it—and her. She must have been coming home."

Frozenly Fleur said, "That broom patch is only four or five hundred feet from the house in a straight line. On a still night it might have been possible— No, no, I know. The widow maker! That's what you heard."

"Widow maker!"

"A broken branch dangling from one of the fir trees at the foot of the west orchard. Lumberjacks call that kind of break a widow maker because sometimes, when such a branch falls, it makes a man's wife his widow. When this one sways, it grinds out a most unearthly groan. We can't do a thing about it—it's too high—except to keep out from under."

She paused, added ruefully, "That's what I meant just now, Nan. We've both been letting our imaginations run riot over something as—as false as a widow maker's groan."

Disturbed and confused, Nan moved restlessly. Fleur, cool, almost cold when she spoke of Huldah. Fleur, emotional and tender when she spoke of David. Yet Huldah had given more than fifty years of her life to this home and family; twenty-eight of them to Fleur herself. At the most, Fleur had known David but three. And now Huldah lay alone in some strange hospital or morgue in Seattle. David, watched over and beloved, in the next room.

"I hope you're right." She tried to speak as coolly as Fleur. "Fleur, let's get out of the house. Brave the elements. Walk around the grounds, at least?"

Fleur shook her head. "It's much too cold. Besides, David will wake soon—want his luncheon. I know. I'll show you what I've done to this floor of the house. Down-stairs has to wait till after the war. I can't get materials—workmen, either. Thor simply did what he could to seal up the great open spaces."

She led Nan on tiptoe through the nursery to a locked door at the end. Turning the key there, she stepped down into a small, cold room, fitted with bunk and drawers, radio, and other equipment to duplicate the cabin of a ship's officer. As trig and neat, too.

"Thor's room now," she explained as she locked the door behind them. "Remember it? Granny's old pressing room. When she died, Thor fixed it up for himself to be near Grandfather and also his back stairs."

"His back stairs?"

"Right here." Fleur opened Thor's door to the corridor, nodded to a narrower one at right angles. It was one of two—Eileen's red door, the other—sealing the end of the hallway.

Nan tried to open the door toward her.

"No, the other way. Otherwise, if left open, it blocks Thor's door."

Pushing the door inward, Nan looked into darkness. Fleur pressed a switch on the stair-well wall, revealing a steep narrow flight of steps, a closed door at their foot, another in the righthand wall.

"Thor's idea, too, and not one of his best. He sliced this passage off the old storeroom. It opens directly into the dining room, or by that side door he can go on down to the basement. He has a shower there. When he comes home at night, he comes in by the basement, showers, then comes up to his room without anyone seeing him."

She snapped off the switch, closed the narrow door. Nan turned to close Thor's.

"No, leave that open, to light the hall. Can you imagine electricians not placing a single light here? It's too maddening. I was away when the house was wired."

Fleur opened the red door. "See what the old store-room's come to."

If Nan hadn't seen Eileen emerge from that doorway, she would have known whose domain lay behind it. Two steps led down into a great room whose steeply slanting ceilings rose to a peak. Once they had looked down on trunks, old furniture, all the family discards of years. Now they and the once unfinished walls were bizarre with plywood painted in broad buff and black stripes. Bright red rugs covered the planked floor, and bright red appeared in odd planes on the modern furniture and shelves. Black and an odd shade of dull blue completed the other spaces.

She stepped down to lift her hands in feigned horror before a canvas on an easel. "Don't tell me that's Washington's sacred cow!" She looked again, amused to find the revered cone of Mount Rainier rising above snowy clouds portrayed as a gelatin mold ringed in whipped cream.

Fleur's nod was brief. When Nan stepped back into the corridor, she closed the door sharply. The first of three doors on the right, she passed with one word: "Huldah's."

One after the other she opened the next two doors, stood back. "I proposed, my guests disposed," she said dryly.

Nan looked first into a large room from which all but essentials had been removed to give it an almost Spartan simplicity. "Beulah's."

The next door—opposite Fleur's—opened as obviously on Mrs. Deven's room. Small ruffled pillows, knitted afghans and robes cluttered the bed and chairs. Framed spiritual mottoes from obscure Hindu philosophers, an elaborate tortoise-shell toilet set, and every size and shape of cosmetic jar crowded the dressing table. Pictures, books, two bronze incense burners, and more Hindu mottoes were stacked in the room's corners.

Fleur waved a hand at them. "She used the room you and Dyke are in for her spiritual exercises. Those are just a few of the properties she required for meditation."

Nan closed that door herself. "What's next?"

Fleur stepped across to her own door, opened it, stood listening. "The one you're in and beside it another where Peggy is, right now. Together, they're supposed to be my guest suite. If you'll stay, I'll arrange it that way again for you and Dyke. That's all except for an extra bathroom across the stair well from my room. Oh, I hear David. Do excuse me, darling. He always expects to see me beside him when he wakes."

She hurried inside. Nan had heard no sound from David, but she made no protest. She remained where she stood until the click of a turning lock recalled her.

The long corridor, lighted only by the window in Thor's room, was dim, almost dark. And still. The stair well, dim, too, led down into stillness.

15

Tuesday Afternoon, January 15

The little clock on the dressing table in her own room told her it was almost two. If she hurried, she could catch the bus at the foot of the hill. Reach Laketon. Meet Dyke, there. Meet Dyke—

In frantic haste she caught up a beret and her coat, pulled them on as she ran down the stairs. But everything worked to oppose her.

She had to struggle with the locked front door. As it flew open under the push of the wind, cold struck her face like a blow. And when she stepped down from the porch, cold sliced like knives at her rayoned ankles.

Nor would the wind, straight from the north, permit her hundred and five pounds to advance against it to the dirt road that ran down to the highway. Hastily to keep it at her back, she turned to follow the walk round the house.

Even then the wind swept her out on the lawn, whirled her round among the old trees, black and stark. As she was rushed along, she caught glimpses of apple and cherry trees in the west orchard, like contorted stakes impaling the cold to the frozen earth.

At their feet a cluster of towering firs tossed high ragged green branches against the wild sky. From one of them the widow maker Fleur had mentioned swayed perilously forty or fifty feet in air. A naked black branch caught over one limb, held there by another.

But her ears caught no sound save the rush of the wind itself. And yesterday there had been no wind!

Suddenly she sprawled headlong across cold rough planks. Her startled eyes looked down through a wide space between two of them on black water far below, still unfrozen but glassy with cold. Awkwardly she forced herself back and scrambled to her feet. She saw then she had fallen across the square, foot-high head of the old well that during Grandfather Wales's regime had served the house. Now platform and pump were gone, replaced by these heavy planks.

Her heart skipped a beat as she visioned the dive into that deep frigid water she might have taken if her fall had shoved those loose boards apart. But the wind, seizing her again, gave her no time to think.

As she spun, she glimpsed Mrs. Bundy in a kitchen window, hands deep in a yellow bowl. And the line of a scarlet sleeve against apple-green curtains in another.

In seconds the house was behind her. With it for a windbreak, she reached the boardwalk and followed it at her own pace to the shelter of the garage, chicken house, and barn. There, warm, almost exhilarated from her tussle with the wind, she paused to catch her breath and survey the frozen world.

Two or three fat, red-feathered hens ran out from a square opening in the chicken-house door to survey her, too. But when she made no response to their inquiring gutturals, clucked themselves inside again.

It was not an inviting world for either hen or her, she thought. Low skies hid everything between her own hill and the crest of the next. Their slopes, brown with wild grass, black with patches of naked woods save where firs and hemlocks showed green, cut arbitrary scallops out of the scudding masses of cloud.

Between the hills lay the main highway, a greasy black ribbon. A single truck hummed along before the wind.

Before her a narrow dirt road led down from the garage to the highway. And across the road a path wound through more brown grass around a low frame structure she remembered as the apple house to a thin line of woods. From them the path leading through and beyond to the village took its name.

To choose between wind-swept highway and more sheltered path was simple. Obsessed with eagerness to reach Laketon and intercept Dyke, she crossed the dirt road.

Shortly she reached the woods, scarcely more than a double line of low trees and underbrush. From them she had a clear view of the hillside and, across massed green at the foot, the gray and sullen expanse of Lake Washington, today jarred with darker bands of pitching waves. And to the west of the trees, the massed roofs of Laketon.

She hurried on, through more wild grass, thin, tall, brittle, brown. Out of it thrust here and there more gnarled skeletons of aged, dying apple trees. And across it, a hundred feet ahead, spread a waving tangle of dark green, long-needled bushes.

She looked at it with surprise, remembering the thin isolated patches of six years ago from which all this had grown. Now it covered hundreds of square feet. And the path was going to lead her right through the center of it.

Altogether the slope was a dreary sight, but for a moment her eyes filled with memories, saw it as she and Fleur had known it in summer when small green apples swelled and grew yellow and red in the sun and cloud shadows played on the fresh green grass. And the Cascades, with Mount Rainier as a climax, rolled majestically along the radiant summer skies.

Suddenly she saw it now as Fleur's—acres and acres of it, running down to the lake—every foot of it with a view of lake and mountains. Its convenience to Seattle—yet its isolation, too! Even she could realize that if after the war Seattle became a city of a million people, this land represented a fortune in real estate.

A light, confidential touch on her arm stopped her. A spray of broom, the long needles cold and hard and sharp, swayed just beside her.

She looked over the green clumps spreading everywhere. Not a solid mass of green, as it had appeared from the woods, but a disorganized wilderness of green shrubs and wild brown grass, broken here and there with scrub fir or apple tree.

The path at her feet lay dark and frozen now, in spots all but hidden by crushed grass. Small wonder that in the dark Huldah had slipped, lost her way.

Her heartbeat quickened as she went on, knowing she must see soon where Huldah had died. She did.

Just where the path curved left around an apple tree, trampled grass began the tragic story. Here men had stumbled in the black and freezing night, lifting Huldah, carrying her out to the path and down to the village.

She tried to assure herself Huldah no longer suffered. But all she could think was how bitterly Grandfather Wales would have condemned such a tragedy if he were alive. But if he were alive, no such tragedy could have occurred.

That, she knew with sudden clarity, was what Fleur was thinking, too!

As understanding flooded her, her own self-condemnation was bitter. It was not concern for David that harassed Fleur. Or self-pity, either. Fleur was miserable, shamed, almost hysterical with grief and remorse—for Huldah! Knowing Fleur so well, how could she have been so blind as not to sense that?

Impelled by remorse herself, she followed the trail into the broom. Perhaps in daylight she could see something, find something, learn something to lessen Fleur's suffering. That horrible boy might have exaggerated, as Dyke had said.

Just inside the first clumps of broom she stopped again, her eyes on the broken grass. Slowly they contracted as the story of Huldah's agonized efforts spelled itself out on the ground.

Round and round and in and out of the broom she had pulled herself by naked, bleeding hands! The path she had broken was broad and irregular. And wherever her hands had gripped the grass, they had left stains to freeze and darken.

Mesmerized by pity, Nan avoided that broken trail. Other feet than hers had avoided it too, she noticed. Men who had come to Huldah's rescue, perhaps, or morbidly curious visitors today had trampled down grass, broken broom branches on all sides in their efforts to remain outside it.

At one spot Huldah must have lain some time. Her hands had groped in all directions!

Blindly Nan turned away, stumbling into and around broom clumps in her haste to break a new trail back to the path.

She stopped. Something had moved beside her. Under her foot.

Looking down, she saw, caught in a little basket of upright grass, a small disk of darker brown. Round and hard. When she picked it up she was little the wiser.

But when she turned it over, her hand shook, almost loosing the bit of light soiled wood. Bloodstains covered it, spread to the roughly rounded edges.

It had dropped, she estimated, less than ten feet from the spot where Huldah had paused so long. But Huldah had not been here. No one had been here. Brown grass stood straight and undisturbed. No broom clump showed a bruised or broken spray.

Yet this wooden disk—button, if the two little holes in its center meant anything—had been in Huldah's hand!

Nan studied it again. A button surely, about the size of a half dollar, carved crudely by someone's hand. A plain, natural-wood button. But plainly not a button that had seen use for many a day.

A gust of wind ran over the broom, sending green ripples tossing southward. She straightened, looked about uneasily. But if her ears had caught some sound her mind had missed, she could not identify it.

Rustling grass and whispering needles. Another truck or car humming along the highway. A dog barking somewhere. All natural sounds, she assured herself.

Nevertheless the cold tingle at the nape of her neck hurried her back to the path. Along it she moved swiftly until the broad red-tiled roofs of the consolidated schools and surrounding roofs of homes and shops were clearly visible just below.

Turning then, she looked back. No one was in sight anywhere on the slope. If it were not for the wooden button in her pocket, she might have imagined those minutes in the broom patch. From that distance it gave no sign that anyone ever visited it or that a path wound through it.

16

Tuesday Afternoon, January 15

A few minutes later in the white-walled waiting room of the small frame bus station Nan felt as if she had stepped through a looking glass. Here was the peaceful humdrum of a wintry village afternoon, made more peaceful still by the ticking of a moonfaced clock on a short counter at one side.

Behind it a gray-haired clerk drooped over a newspaper in the wilting breath of a potbellied iron stove. Two or three waiting passengers were somnolent near by in wide-armed chairs. Not a sound save the ticking of the clock, yet how different from the stillness at Madrona Place!

Her body soaked up heat and quiet like a turtle on a sunny log. But her mind resembled nothing so much as one of those artificial snowstorms inside a glass ball where the flakes whirl to drift and settle in a formless pattern about a central figure as the glass gradually clears.

Thoughts, impressions, bits of memories. . . . Those groanlike sounds she and Dyke had heard as they approached the house . . . lights flashing off and on . . . Mrs. Devens's reluctant welcome . . . Fleur's . . . Eileen's . . . Beulah's . . . bruises on Fleur's throat . . . Huldah's signature . . . that sly Prentiss boy's pleasure in the news he brought . . . running feet on the boardwalk . . . Dyke watching in freezing darkness at a window . . . David sleeping on a living-room couch . . . Eileen's two-pronged words . . . Eileen telling of her life, Ruby's, Beulah's . . . Beulah's prying questions . . . Fleur's love for David . . . Fleur's fears for David . . . the widow maker . . . that houseful of women, linked only by the name of Wales . . . the cold . . . stillness . . . isolation . . . not even a telephone. . . .

Above all, Huldah . . . Huldah dying alone, in pain, in the cold darkness . . . the broom patch . . . the button . . . the button in her pocket. . . .

Perhaps because her fingers still held tightly to that button, the drifting fragments of her thoughts were drawn to settle about it, relate themselves to it. But formlessly. Try as she would she could find no unifying explanation in it for the events of the past twenty hours.

Yet without conscious effort one impression grew clearer, stronger by contrast with the warm peace of the bus station. No matter what happened at Madrona Place, fear came first!

The two-thirty and three o'clock busses from Seattle arrived and went their way. Dyke was not on either of them. Before another half-hour ticked by, she had formulated and discarded several theories. And reached one decision.

She and Dyke must not remain another night at Madrona Place!

Even Huldah whose letter had brought Dyke West had realized he must not come there. She must have told him to remain in Seattle, that she would bring her information to him there. That would account for his obstinacy about leaving the city. That would account for Huldah's determination to go to Cranford on Saturday.

She could reach Seattle from Cranford easily and without knowledge of the Barnacles at Madrona Place. Among the Barnacles, Nan now included Eileen and, with reservations, Peggy.

Without the knowledge of the Barnacles! Her mind fixed on those words. And on Fleur's: "I'm a prisoner in my own house!"

Fleur had denied that later, but what if it were true? She had refused to leave the house—leave David alone—even to walk about the grounds. While showing Nan the upper floor, she had remained always in the corridor where she could watch her own door. And though David had made no sound, she had hurried back to him, locking her door behind her.

What if Huldah had been a prisoner, too! The idea was fantastic. But no more fantastic than that Huldah should have tried to take David away in the middle of the night! Should have escaped herself in the darkness of the early morning—

Escaped!

Her thoughts whirled round that word, finally ranged themselves in an explanation.

Fleur had lied—to protect David, to protect Huldah and last of all herself. Huldah would never have entered Fleur's room like that, tried to take David away. Her whole life had been devoted to Fleur, to saving her, guarding her from even the smallest unpleasantnesses.

Someone else—not Huldah—had tried to take David away. And Huldah had escaped—not to Cranford, but to Seattle—to wait for Dyke. Huldah had sent for Dyke to save Fleur!

To save Fleur from the Barnacles! To save Madrona Place, too.

Nan's heart turned over, and she sat for a time numb with self-reproach.

What if Huldah had waited somewhere in Seattle until Monday—the first day Dyke could arrive if he left New

York immediately? What if she had gone to the Grandview
Monday afternoon—only to find he had left for Madrona
Place? What if, in her haste to get back there, she had tak-
en the first bus to Laketon, hurried up that slippery path,
fallen—

Memory of those dreadful sounds she and Dyke had
heard on the tiled walk brought strange comfort. If Huldah
had been their source, then she couldn't have visited the
Grandview. She couldn't possibly have done so and reached
Laketon by bus, the broom patch on foot, by the time
their taxi stopped at the madrona tree.

Those awful moments of realizing her own guilt in
forcing Dyke to leave the Grandview, however, moved Nan
to make a solemn vow with herself. After this she'd never
again interfere with Dyke's plans. Never! No matter what
the cost to herself.

Yet she must get him away from Madrona Place. Fleur,
too. And David, she conceded reluctantly, knowing that
without him Fleur could never be persuaded.

Perhaps Dyke had already found a place for them. Perhaps that was why he was so long in coming. No matter
how modest a roof it was, she would make it a comfortable
and untroubled haven for all of them.

The plan fairly reeked with good sense. Yet even as she
admired it, she knew a guilty feeling of offering hostages
to fortune. It was what she so passionately wanted for
herself!

Movement in the room about her, clouds of steam bil-
lowing against the windows from the hood of a short-
ing bus outside, roused her. Drugged with heat and her
thoughts, she sped for the door.

At the bus she scanned the windows, trying to see each
face inside at once. One held her gaze. A lean, dark-faced
man's, framed in newspaper. A man so angry she could

feel his anger boring into and through her like white-hot flame.

He was unaware of her as he gazed out over her head at nothing, his eyes narrowed to slits beneath the brim of his own downdrawn fedora. His lips set so hard that muscles made small bunches at the corners of his mouth, carved deep grooves in his cheeks. She tore her eyes away, turned to circle the bus on the other side.

As she moved, the man moved too. His newspaper flew into the air. Signaling violently to her, he leaped to his feet. Dyke!

While she still gazed unbelievingly at the bus window, he burst out the opened door. She took a step toward him, stopped, more incredulous than ever.

His eyes were clear now, his white teeth flashing as he smiled. Before the gaze of interested passengers, he caught her up, kissed her soundly, set her down. Then, an arm about her shoulders, he looked about.

"Ah! There it is, the tavern in the town." He waved his free arm expansively, propelled her rapidly across the street with the other. "You shall have a drink, wonderful."

With a flourish he threw, open the door to a long, brightly lighted room. Down one side ran a counter, complete with mirrors and a solitary attendant. Down the other, half a dozen high-backed booths. No customers were visible as they passed by. Dyke selected the one at the end with a juke box beside it, bowed her in.

"Daiquiri, as usual? Sandwiches?"

He left her, returned, one hand filled with nickels. Before he joined her, he contributed one to each of the slots in the machine's entire repertoire. As it burst raucously into action, he flung himself down beside her.

She inspected him anxiously. "You're all right? Nothing's wrong?"

Two glasses of beer and thick ham sandwiches slid onto the table before them from the counterman's tin tray.

"Plenty's wrong. I asked for daiquiris."

"Are you kidding?" the waiter demanded. "This ain't no club. Beer's all you get in this state, stranger. 'Less you buy the makings, take 'em home."

"It's all right." Nan waved the man away impatiently, turned to Dyke. "What's really wrong?"

"On the contrary." Dyke lifted his glass to her. "What I came out here to do, Nan, isn't a patch on what I'm going to do. Thanks to you, hon. I can't tell you much, but this I can say. I had to see a lawyer named Henrickson this morning. When I entered his office his greeting was simply run-of-the-mine. To him I was a very junior member of an eastern firm sent out on a minor mission. But when he learned where I spent the night, where my toothbrush and wife rested at that very moment, ah, then the keys of the city were presented, with bows. That's all, my little one, except that your wish is granted. We stay and stay and stay with Fleur."

Somehow she kept her eyes shining and expectant. But dismay boiled within her, threatened to burst from her lips against her will. Was it only a moment ago she'd made that promise to herself never again to interfere with Dyke's plans?

"Don't look so wide-eyed yet. I've still got to see what can be done."

Nan reached for her beer, lifted it slowly to him. It was the best she could do to applaud him and conceal the disappointment settling over her like a weight.

He was not deceived. "What's the matter, hon? You look pretty well upset in spite of those all-for-dear-old-Rutgers smiles."

"Can I ask one question?"

"If I don't have to answer it."

"If you're so pleased over this new development, why did you look like the world's maddest man, sitting in that bus? I didn't even recognize you."

His face hardened. "I'd rather not go into that. It hasn't been an easy day. For one thing, I walked down to Laketon to get the bus this morning. Saw that broom patch. For another, Mrs. Devens was on the bus when it reached the village. I had the pleasure of a long talk with her."

He thrust his brief case further away from them on the table. "Forget it. What about you?"

"I came down by the woods path, too."

"You did? Nan, I wish you wouldn't do things like that."

"Why?"

"Why? Because it's slippery and treacherous."

"I didn't find it so." In spite of her intention to be calm, a tingle came into her voice.

"No?" He looked at her hard. "What did you find?"

She hesitated, then extracted the wooden button from her pocket, placed it on the table before him.

He didn't touch it. "Where'd you get that?"

"In the broom patch."

"How'd you find it when I saw nothing? Or the police either, evidently. I met a couple of them coming up the path as I went down."

"This wasn't—anywhere near the place where Huldah'd been. Or anyone else. The grass wasn't broken at all where I found it."

"Could have been dropped there any time by anyone, couldn't it? Looks pretty old and weather-beaten to me."

"It had been in Huldah's hand."

"How do you know?"

In answer, she turned the button over.

He looked at the dark stains there, his face noncommittal. "Why would she throw it away?"

"I wondered about that, too. Perhaps she thought no one would think anything of it if it were found in her purse or pocket. It seems to me she must have thrown it deliberately. To have it found. Make someone notice it."

"She took a big chance. It might never have been found."

"Well, then, perhaps that's why she threw it. She didn't want it found. Was afraid someone would notice it. Either way, I'm sure it means something."

"Anyone around when you found it?"

She hesitated. "I don't think so. I didn't see anyone."

He moved the little round base of his glass about, tracings circles on the table top. Suddenly he turned to her. "Could be it means something—"

The glass slipped from his fingers, crashed to the floor. While Nan wiped beer from her sleeve, he stooped to look under the table. When he straightened, he announced, "One complete casualty. Let's have another, shall we, while you bring me up to date on Madrona Place today?"

As the counterman approached, Dyke picked up the button, dropped it in his pocket.

Nan could be noncommittal too. "Oh, nothing much—unless you'd be interested to know that Eileen says I'm the wrong Holliman."

She knew she had startled him, but he said lightly, "Meaning I'm the right one? File that thought for reference, my wife. I must have words with Eileen."

"I don't think you need to bother. Ruby Devens probably told you what Eileen told me. Just my luck to draw the supersubtle one. You'd have understood what she was saying, but I'm just beginning now to figure it out."

She stopped. He was grinning at her. "Lord, you're a quick learner. Keep away from Eileen, will you? Meantime, break that down for me."

"Why—I mean the land. Fleur's land. That's why they're all here, isn't it? To try to take it—or most of it—away from her?"

"Whew!" He whistled. "Begin at the beginning, will you? Tell me exactly what she said—"

Almost word for word, Nan repeated Eileen's stories. "Nothing in that to justify your assumption," he commented when she finished.

"Not in the words alone. But there was her voice too. And the way she looked as she talked. Just too, too naive—for a woman who says herself she's sophisticated. She doesn't believe in coincidences. And neither do I—in this case. I think she was telling me—for you, through me— that all the money the Wales boys and girls invested in land was invested in Madrona Place. I think that's why they all resent Fleur—why they act as if they had every right to be in Fleur's home. And I think that's why she's afraid of them."

"You've missed a step somewhere, assuming for a moment that you know what you're talking about. If they have claims, there must be records—"

"Oh!" Nan cried. "That's what I mean. There can't be records. They're cooking this up—I don't know the right words."

"Will 'conspiring to defraud' do?"

She nodded. "Nicely."

"And you've identified the 'they'?"

"Eileen, Ruby, Beulah, of course. Perhaps not Peggy, though she may be acting for her mother."

"And Fleur's afraid of them? You'd better tell me about that, too. About your whole day, Nan."

Detail by detail he drew from her everything she had seen and done and heard from the moment she opened her door at half past, eleven until she reached the bus station almost three hours later. When she finished, he drank his second beer slowly and in silence.

"Well?" she prodded, finally. Hope sparkled inside her. Surely he'd feel too now they should leave Madrona Place, take Fleur with them—and quickly.

"Well—you must remember, hon, you were very tired when we reached Madrona Place yesterday. Pretty well wrought up emotionally, weren't you, over one thing or another?"

"You can't think I imagined all this!"

"No. But it's possible to misinterpret—be mistaken, isn't it?" He looked at her gravely. "Do you think you could just be Mrs. Dyke Holliman, visiting her old friend, Fleur Wales?"

"Mind my own business, you mean?"

"Temporarily. If you don't mind." He looked at his wrist watch. "Almost five. Want to wait here while I run into the post office? I'll be back in two minutes."

Blandly he rose, picked up her coat and held it for her. Then, shaking himself into his own, he strode off to settle his account.

She watched him go thoughtfully. Then, fishing a compact from her pocket, sat down to make up her lips with leisured care. But her wits were racing. Everything was clicking into place.

Dyke had not denied or laughed off her idea about that "conspiracy to defraud." He had listened carefully, hardly concealing his interest, drawn every word Eileen had said from her. Fleur's, too.

Huldah would have ferreted out this conspiracy very shortly after the Barnacles began to arrive. And since their arrivals dated from last spring, she must have tried first to defeat it herself. Failing, she had sent for Dyke.

Perhaps that was why she had been kept from going to Cranford, why she'd had to get away in the dark of early morning escape!

Someone must have seen or learned of that letter Huldah had sent Dyke. Eileen? Eileen didn't consider their arrival a coincidence!

And who could have been a more logical choice to turn to than Dyke? Dyke was a lawyer. Dyke, if not by blood, by marriage ties, was Fleur's half brother. Dyke was the husband of Fleur's best friend.

And Dyke had come. And Huldah was dead. . . .

She found herself looking into a pair of terrified eyes in the little mirror of her compact. Her own eyes!

"All set?" Dyke's voice asked at her elbow.

She closed the compact slowly, returned it to her pocket, rose.

"All set," she heard herself say steadily.

But inwardly she was far from set. She had offered hostages to fortune. And they had been refused.

Now she must return to Madrona Place—to that still house where, no matter what happened, fear came first.

17

Tuesday Evening, January 15

Their arrival at Madrona Place undermined her ripening forebodings. As they stepped down from the village taxi at the madrona, the blue dimout lamp winked almost cheerily through the thick dusk. Both screen and house doors were unlocked. And they looked into a living room not only lighted and warm but somehow rearranged to reduce its effect as a battlefield of unfortunate tastes.

Their own room, too, showed changes. A robust little stove replaced the electric heater. Its warm breath reached even to the far corners of the bathroom. At a touch, hot water poured from taps and shower.

"You see, Nan? Everything's under control. Fleur will pull herself together now she knows definitely about Huldah. It was the uncertainty that threw her—"

"Then you didn't see any marks on her throat? Your brief case wasn't disturbed?"

"I'm willing to accept her explanation for those bruises. And I could be mistaken about the folders. You weren't the only one tired and irritable, ready to suspect and believe the worst, when we arrived here yesterday."

"Yes, dear," she said sweetly and took refuge behind cold cream.

He started to speak, thought better of it. But as he rummaged in his traveling bag, he used only his hands. His eyes never left her face.

When he had departed for a shower, Nan sank down on the dressing-table bench, her fingers moving automatically. She felt confused, uncertain what to believe or think. Anxious and vexed with Dyke, too. Yet in that bus station, in the tavern, too, everything had seemed so clear.

In New York she willingly played up to Dyke's idea that she was a young, inexperienced creature, utterly dependent on him.

A being set apart from the world of criminal law and law courts in which he spent his days. Under that masterful delusion he had progressed rapidly in the firm of Rensselaer, Struthers, and Bayles during the three years they had been married.

But here in this strangely changed house she had not only Dyke but Fleur to consider. Her plan to get them both away from Madrona Place had failed. And yet, if that thought that sprang at her from her compact mirror had basis in fact, she must get them away.

Huldah had tried to protect Fleur. Now she was dead. And Dyke had taken her place!

A light flashed on in her mind. Was that why Fleur wanted Dyke at Madrona Place? Did she know—suspect, at least—that Huldah's death was no accident?

Dyke appearing at that moment gave her no more time to think. Only time to finish dressing quickly and descend with him to the living room as if they were really just guests in the home of an old friend.

Thor, mixing himself a highball at the small black walnut table, looked up as they entered. "Just in time, strangers. I'll make it four. Fleur'll be here any minute."

"Good lord! Let me do that," Dyke exclaimed. "Sit down, Thor. You look as if you'd been drawn through a knothole."

"That's one way of putting it," Thor admitted wearily. "I spent most of the day in Seattle."

Nan turned to look at him as he followed her to the fire. He walked heavily, wore an emptied look. And curiously, he looked younger, too, like—like an exhausted young track runner, she finally decided. When Dyke gave him his drink, he didn't wait, drank it immediately, all of it.

"I needed that," he said to Nan in apology.

Fleur arriving then cut off any explanation, held the attention of all as she moved down the long room toward them.

Watching her, Nan thought of the stately Fleur she had been so proud of in college. Now in a long black wool house gown, her shining black, hair rolled back, her oval face beautifully smooth though pale, she looked positively regal.

"Well?" she said as she stopped before them.

"Well!" they chorused in appreciation. "Well, well!"

She smiled, coloring with pleasure, and took her drink from the tray Dyke presented with a flourish.

Gradually, as they sat about the fire in relaxed and comfortable silence, it dawned on Nan that she was the only one taking the scene at face value. Fleur and Thor, she could see now, were building up to something. For that matter, so was Dyke.

Fleur smiled at her, turned to Dyke. "I'm not fooling your wife, and I hope I'm not fooling you. I'm just trying to make up for my sins of yesterday and to persuade you and Nan to stay with me for as long as you're to be in Seattle."

"I'm on my best behavior, too," Dyke assured her, "and for the same reason. There isn't much chance of securing even a hotel room for weeks."

"Good. Then you'll stay."

Nan, watching and listening with mingled emotions, was unaware until he spoke that Thor was watching her.

"The gossip is," he told her solemnly, "that you ap-peared like a Valkyrie in the village this afternoon and dragged your husband off a bus into the tavern. Tchk! Tchk! Such goings on!"

"And I saw nary a spy."

"Laketon's full of eyes and ears. I stopped off there on my way home from Seattle. Picked up the news note with the whisky."

"I had to go south and Laketon was in the way—so I waited for Dyke to finance a taxi home."

"I hope you took the woods path. That highway's no place for a bantamweight in a wind."

She nodded. "I saw the place where they found Huldah."

"So did I. Early this morning." The light went out of his face again. "That reminds, me I must cultivate your husband. What's the etiquette of approaching the law? I know there are lawyers and lawyers. Which kind is he?"

"Good or bad? Criminal or civil?"

"I know he's civil. But perhaps a lawyer who knows about crime is what we need."

"We?" Dyke pricked up his ears. "And what crime?"

"We means this whole house, I guess. But whether there's been a crime and if so, whose—" Thor's shoulders moved wearily; he began again. "I spent most of the day in the County Courthouse in Seattle, answering the district attorney's questions. It seems he—and the county coroner—feel some doubt about how Huldah died. From the questions, I thought perhaps we'd better be prepared."

"For what?"

"Maybe nothing. The coroner found Huldah's death was caused by a heart spasm. Coronary thrombosis. But he questions other conditions."

"Such as?"

"She'd fallen, broken her hip, for one thing."

"That could have happened to anyone, on that path. Even in daylight."

"She was badly scratched and bruised."

"Nothing strange about that—the way she dragged and bumped around in that broom and dried grass. Those brittle stalks have an edge like a knife."

"They admit all that. The main thing is a bad blow on the forehead. Near her in the broom was a piece of old apple-tree branch. The tree itself is in that broom patch, right beside the path. One explanation is that it may already have been hanging and she bumped into it in the dark. It fell when she did, and she carried it along with her as a cane."

"That's pretty fancy figuring."

"If they'd found bits of its bark in the wound, it would be still fancier," Thor assured him grimly.

"They think that branch may have been used as a weapon?"

"It's not a large branch, not much more than an inch thick. And old, dead wood. Not heavy enough if she knocked against it to give her a really serious blow. And something had struck her—hard."

As Dyke started, to speak, Thor corrected himself hastily. "Don't get me wrong. They didn't make any statements. Just—just asked questions that suggested they were considering both an accidental death and—murder."

"Murder!" Nan cried, stopped aghast at the relief she heard in her voice. She was relieved to have that ugly word said aloud.

No one heard her. A crash of notes from the piano jerked all their heads around.

Mrs. Devens stood there, one hand pressed down on the keys for support. The other was doubled in a fist against her mouth. As they gazed at her, speechless, she opened that hand to smooth it back over her face and hair in an incredible effort at nonchalance.

"Dinner," she murmured. "Dinner is ready, Fleur." Turning, she fairly scuttled from the room.

Fleur rose at once. "We'll talk later," she told Dyke. "Now we'd better go. I don't think she'll repeat what she overheard—if anything, but—"

"Why not tell them all yourself, Fleur?" he recommended. "Or let Thor or me. Then if the D.A. comes round with questions—"

"Unless it's necessary, I don't want them alarmed at all."

She slipped a hand through Nan's arm, drew her ahead toward the sitting-room door.

"I heard you tell Thor you saw the—broom patch," she said as they went. "I wish I'd gone with you, Nan. There might have been— Somehow I keep thinking Huldah would have tried to leave something for me—"

Nan started to speak, then closed her lips, shook her head.

18

Tuesday Evening, January 15

Dinner progressed with surprising smoothness, the unusual weather providing an invaluable source of conversation. When it was exhausted, Eileen unaccountably began to tell tales of Africa.

Only Mrs. Devens was silent. She picked at her food, eating nothing.

In the middle of a sentence Eileen turned to her. "I'm afraid you acquired another of your headaches in town today, Ruby."

"No. I—" Mrs. Devens looked up, her face pasty white and puffy, her small rouged mouth an incongruous spot of color in it. "You must excuse me, Eileen. I was thinking of my own affairs, I'm afraid."

Smiling tightly, she turned to Fleur. "I think I've found my little house, at last."

"Ruby, that's splendid. However, before you decide don't you think you should have someone go over it with you, give you a professional opinion about it?"

"It's been rented furnished for the past year. It's just now available. I—I can rent it for a month, with an option to buy it if I like it. That is, if I take it right away."

"Where is it?" Thor asked.

"In the Magnolia district. Just a small place, and not new. I told the agent I'd move in tomorrow, Fleur. I'll just take a few personal things, of course, until I decide. I hope that won't incon—"

She jumped as Peggy broke in sharply, "Listen. I hear a car stopping."

Thor rose. "Sounds like it. I'll go."

Mrs. Devens pushed her chair back. "Will you excuse me, Fleur? I have so many things to do."

"But you've eaten nothing, Ruby," Beulah pointed out. "And if you don't eat now, you know you will later. So you'll save no time."

Thor spoke from the kitchen door. "It's Jud LaRue, Fleur."

"Bring him in here," Fleur instructed calmly. "Jud's an old friend," she told the others when Thor had gone. "For years he was Grandfather Wales' right-hand man. Then we lost sight of him for years more. Until he popped up in politics. Two years ago he was elected sheriff."

She turned, smiling, as Thor led in a broad, heavy, awkward man. A mackinaw about his shoulders, gray flannel, tieless shirt, corduroy trousers laced into high boots, and an ear-lugged wool cap in his hand suggested a lumberjack more than a political official.

He walked slowly toward Fleur, embarrassment written all over him. And turned on the table as he came, round eyes the flat opaque blue of small boys' 'crocky' marbles. So much like crockies, Nan thought, it was difficult to read expression in them.

"Good evening, Miss Fleur," he said in a slurred drawl. "I'm sorry to come breaking in like this."

"Don't be. It's about time you came to see us, Jud. Thor and are among your faithful supporters. You'll have coffee with us, of course."

She nodded to Peggy, then introduced the sheriff to her household. Under that blue gaze, Mrs. Devens sat down as if someone had placed a weight on her head.

"Sit by me, Jud," Thor invited, placing a chair. "You can see I need reinforcements occasionally."

The sheriff lowered himself uncomfortably and fumbled with his cap, finally hooking it over the back of his chair.

"Yes, I see." His eyes went round the table again. "You got quite a family now, Miss Fleur. But this ain't a social call, folks."

Tension tightened about the table as he hitched his chair forward. "Now don't be upset, Miss Fleur. May be nothing in this at all. But the D.A.'s raised some questions about Huldah Swenson's death."

Silence. Thor broke it, to say, "I've told Fleur and the Hollimans, too, about the questions he asked me."

"You didn't tell us when Huldah's death occurred," Dyke said. "Do you know, Sheriff?"

The blue eyes shifted to him. "She'd been dead at least forty-eight hours when founds the coroner says."

Nan's constricted lungs let out a tuck. Then Huldah had been dead before she and Dyke arrived in Seattle! Huldah couldn't have gone to the Grandview Monday afternoon.

"The low temperatures we've been having lately make it pretty hard to say much more than that," the sheriff was continuing. "She could have died as early as six or seven o'clock Saturday morning or up to eight or so Saturday night. It would be dark both those times, and it must have been dark when she fell. Otherwise she'd have been able to see her way, pulled herself within calling distance of this house."

He sighed gustily. "Too bad it was Saturday and so cold. Any other day kids might of found her on their way to school or the movies."

"You believe she died Saturday morning then," Dyke said quickly.

"That's my personal opinion." LaRue appeared abashed for a moment, changed the subject. "Huldah was a wonderful old woman. Proud and independent as Lucifer. Liked things done respectably. Tod bad she had to go that way. I've just a few questions, folks."

"Would you rather talk to us one at a time?" Thor asked.

"No. Guess the quickest way to get this over is to ask them with you all sitting in. You'll know the truth, and I'll ask you to tell me here—or later—if any of you hear anything said that isn't true. First question is—which of you had any reason to want an old woman like Huldah out of your way?"

A circle of horrified faces answered him. No one spoke.

Nan's was as horrified as the rest. At his stupidity in asking such a question with everyone present. How could he expect to learn anything that way? But if he had asked her alone, she could have told him. Three, four people at that table, if Peggy were included, had reason to wish Huldah out of the way. Two of them had actually admitted to her their relief that Huldah was dead.

She tried to catch the sheriff's eye. But he wasn't looking at her, at anyone, apparently. Just sitting there like a dolt, nodding his head!

"The D.A. thinks it needs explaining why none of you looked for her," he was drawling now. "Why none of you found her where she was, within four hundred feet of this house. You knew Saturday morning sometime she was gone, didn't you?"

"Of course we did," Beulah told him brusquely. "Though not till almost noon. She'd had a bad night. My room's right next to hers. And I heard her moving round for most of it. So when she didn't come down in the morning, we thought she was sleeping, didn't disturb her."

"She'd talked all week about going to her cottage at Cranford, Jud," Fleur said then. "I'd told her Thor would drive her over Saturday afternoon if she insisted on going in this weather. But she was very independent, as you said. And we didn't know till late Saturday afternoon, when Thor came back from taking over food and extra blankets, that she hadn't gone there."

"I went twice Sunday, too," Thor added gloomily. "It's easy to see now we should have looked for her—gone down that path at least. But Huldah was such a strong old woman. I guess it never occurred to any of us—I know it didn't to me—that she might have met with an accident."

"Yeah, I know." The sheriff shifted his weight. "These aren't my questions. I'm asking for the D.A. He wants to know why you didn't report her missing."

The faces round the table were almost as horrified as at his first question.

"The answer to that, Sheriff," Eileen's low voice said, "is that we were never aware she was missing. Whether she stood before us in the flesh or not, we were always conscious of her. Even if we'd thought to notify the police, I doubt if we would have dared. We'd have been in fear of our lives of her outraged pride when she returned. Certainly I did nothing, but then, I never do."

LaRue wrinkled his forehead trying to follow her, gave up.

Peggy at his elbow leaned forward unhappily. "I'm partly to blame, Mr. LaRue. Huldah said one day last week she was going into Seattle soon, to see some people there. Sometimes she told me things she didn't tell others. I didn't mention that until Thor came back Sunday afternoon from Cranford. Then I suggested she might have gone into Seattle. I thought she had."

"I told the D.A.," the sheriff said then, "it wasn't likely any Wales would find cause now for turning on a woman who'd been as good as a member of the family for more than fifty years."

Relieved of that long sentence, he leaned back. "Next question is—how about the neighbors? Any of them have any grudge against her? She spoke her mind pretty freely, as I remember very well."

"We have no neighbors. You know that, Jud," Fleur reminded. "Huldah was always most courteous and hospitable to guests."

"That's right. Well, then, what about prowlers? You're 'way off here alone—vacant land on all sides. Except for Wales Center. It draws plenty of people. Some of them might think of coming up here—"

"Nonsense!" Beulah snapped at him. "This section's law-abiding as a church."

"Used to be," he corrected. "But this country's full of war workers these days, and there's all sorts among 'em. All sorts of people here, too, to prey on 'em. On the money they're making, I mean."

"Who'd hang around that woods path—especially, on a cold dark morning or evening—on the chance of someone coming along?" Thor scoffed. "Even on weekdays no one but a few school kids go that way. Once in a while someone from this house."

"How about this Prentiss kid?" the sheriff asked. "He comes from a big family of no-accounts. Just over the next hill. He says—and it's true—that two of their heifers broke out last Monday afternoon while everyone was away. But it seems funny, don't it, that he'd be over here hunting them in the dark? Stumble into that broom patch, find Huldah? He might have been over here Saturday, too. Huldah ever have any trouble with him, with any of them?"

"No. If he wanted to try to trip or heave a rock at anyone in this house," Thor assured him, "I'd be his mark. He and I meet regularly spring and fall when he comes over to steal cherries and apples. Last fall I told him he was a big boy, now—that next time I'd do more than warn him off the place."

The sheriff thrust back his untouched coffee, lumbered to his feet, "I was just asking," he said again, and there was authority in his voice he hadn't shown before, "in case it looked like we ought to have an inquest. I guess that won't be necessary. The body'll be released to you in the morning, Miss Fleur."

19

Tuesday Night, January 15

Silence held the table until Thor returned from accompanying the sheriff to the door. He took his chair quietly enough, but even before he spoke the resolution in his face spoke for him.

"Huldah's dead," he said slowly. "We can't bring her back. And we can't go on like this either—each of us blaming himself or someone else for what's happened. We're all to blame. What we've got to do now is to see nothing like this happens again."

He paused to choose his words. "If it hadn't been that Jud LaRue knew Madrona Place so well—and Huldah's life here—we might be facing a very difficult investigation. It looks odd to more than the district attorney that Huldah could leave this house and nothing be done or said about it for three days."

"LaRue say that?" Dyke wanted to know.

Thor nodded uncomfortably. "Laketon's changed—and the country all about us. All sorts of new people have moved in. We've been so busy with our own affairs, we've had no time to think about them. There's a Civilian Defense Office in the village, and a very active Red Cross Center. And a Recreation Center for the two army camps on the lake. They're all run by women. Without the help of anyone in this house."

"Quote, unquote?" Eileen asked.

"Yes. And Jud said something else. Naturally Madrona Place and Fleur are well known to all the old residents in this part of the country. But they haven't seen her, heard from her for months. Jud says they're curious and critical, but not nearly so much as the newcomers."

"Gossip!" Beulah was complacently contemptuous. "Let them. The Wales choose their own friends, go their own way."

"That wasn't Grandfather Wales' way. He knew everyone and everyone knew him. And that hasn't been Fleur's way—until the last few months. The result is, Jud says, that feeling in Laketon is pretty strong against Madrona Place for the way Huldah died. If there had been an investigation, we'd have had little support or sympathy from anyone around here. On the contrary—"

"But Thor, I've been so busy," Fleur protested. "I simply haven't been able to go about as I used to, have people here."

"If the phone had been in order, you could have called them or they could have reached you. That's just—just a small thing, but we can do something about it right away. I'm going to see the phone company in the morning when I go into Seattle. Tell them to go ahead."

"We told them that months ago. They've done nothing," Fleur reminded him. "You know I even offered to pay any additional charges to have the wires brought in from the back road."

"And they refused. It's too bad, Fleur. I know how you feel about those trees, especially the madrona. Now they'll have to come down."

"No. I'll never agree to that. Never!" Fleur sat erect, her voice firm. "Grandfather Wales planted those trees himself, named this place for the madrona. It's the only one I have."

"The only one we have, Fleur." Thor was looking straight at her, his determination as inflexible as hers.

Electricity flashed through the silence now. Fleur sat motionless a moment, then tried to speak. But no words came from her moving lips.

Thor did not take his eyes from her. Waiting.

"Not yet, Thor." Fleur's words were hardly audible.

"Now."

"I can't. You know I can't. Yet."

"I can."

As he spoke, Fleur rose unsteadily swayed. Dyke leaped to his feet, caught her as she fell. But when he turned to place her on a couch, Thor moved round the table swiftly.

"I'll take her." He lifted Fleur easily, moved for the door.

Peggy was there, opening it. When she closed it, she was on the other side, following Thor.

"Well!" Beulah exclaimed angrily. "The idea of Thor talking like that to Fleur. At a time like this. That young man should be put in his place."

"After all, Thor owes a great deal to Huldah," Dyke suggested. "And no one's given much thought to how he is feeling."

"If you'll excuse me—" Eileen rose, her eyes bright. Walking over to the little door to the back stairs, she opened it, then paused to smile back at Dyke. "It looks as if he were about to take it."

The door closed behind her, and they heard her light footsteps mounting the stairs. When the upper door opened and closed, Mrs. Devens pushed back her chair.

"I really must go, too." She hurried to the backstairs door, murmuring something about much to do.

"All this nonsense about a tree!" Beulah went on as if neither Eileen nor Ruby had spoken. "With a world at war, they fight over a tree."

"I take it trees must come down to bring a telephone in," Dyke prompted. "But you have a phone—"

"Much good it does us! The whole thing's a tempest in a teapot. The phone company insists the line must run along the front road because one day that will be a main street. Fleur wants the wires brought in from the back. When they wouldn't agree to that, she compromised by having those trees along the road topped. But that was two or three years ago, and they've grown out again and interfere with the wires. The phone people refuse to repair the line until the madrona comes down and the rest are topped again."

"Wires can be brought in underground," Dyke said.

"When they don't even do that in Seattle, there's not much chance of it here."

"But Thor's right," Nan declared. "You should have a phone." Her lips burned with questions, but from Dyke's manner she knew she couldn't ask them. Not then.

"Why don't you get some rest, too, Mrs. Bundy?" she suggested instead. "You must be awfully tired. Dyke and I will take care of everything, put the house to bed."

Beulah rose, proud of her vigor. "You and Dyke run along. And don't worry about me. With Ruby leaving tomorrow, my fingers are simply itching to get at that kitchen."

In the living room Nan demanded immediately, "What did Thor mean by that 'we'? Do you think Grandfather Wales could have left him an interest in this place?"

"Could be," Dyke said absently. He had stopped to look down at the highball tray on the little walnut table. She moved back to see what held his attention. A soda bottle, a bowl half full of melted ice, and three highball glasses were there.

"Where's the other?" she asked, looking round. "There should be four."

"With the whisky, I suppose. It's gone, too."

He picked up the tray, carried it out to the kitchen. While he was gone, she rescued the lamp, a hand-painted cow's horn, on a rosewood base, a small vase of artificial flowers and the heavy brass desk wedge from the top of a bookcase, replaced them on the table. And prepared another question.

When Dyke returned, she asked it. "What did Eileen mean about Thor taking his place?"

Dyke threw himself into a chair, lighted a cigarette. "Well, she's an artist, isn't she? Must have studied anatomy. Knows about bones."

"Bones?"

"Everyone has bones," he informed her and would say no more. As she smoked her own cigarette, she watched him through her lashes, trying to guess his thoughts. No one had mentioned Jud LaRue and the purpose of his visit, but from the way Dyke gazed into the fire, she felt sure he was going over those questions and answers, word by word.

"Imagine that Jud LaRue a sheriff," she tried tentatively. "Why, he couldn't—"

She was more successful than she wished to be. He tossed his cigarette into the fire, turned on her.

"All right. Let's have it. You believe Huldah was murdered, don't you? You were practically bursting to tell LaRue not only how it was done, but who did it, weren't you? Then prove it. With facts. Not guesses. Who? How? Where? When? Why? With what?"

Challenged, she went over each question in her mind. Not to a single one could she give a definite answer. Only suspicions, guesses, impressions.

She sat up, irked by the smile with which he was watching her.

"The legal mind! Honestly, dear, sometimes I wish I'd married a farmer or—or something. Anyone can think if he has all the facts in his hands. It's much more difficult when you haven't."

His roar of laughter stopped short. The room had gone dark except for the immediate glow of the coals before them.

She called quickly, imitating Fleur, "It's all right, Beulah. We're still here."

When the darkness continued, Dyke rose. Halfway to the curtains, he stopped. The lights had come on again, not in the lamps, in the ceiling cluster.

He looked at the lamps that had gone out, up at the cluster. Then strode to the curtains, threw them open. No one was in the foyer or on the stairs. The door to the kitchen was closed. When he opened it, he looked into darkness.

Returning, he found Nan gazing oddly at the black walnut table.

"Look, Dyke," she said shakily. "That brass desk gadget is gone. And I—I put it there myself just a few minutes ago."

20

Tuesday Night, January 15

In their room Dyke began to arrange the armchair in the window, equip it with a blanket, flashlight, his watch.

"You're not going to sit in that freezing window again," she protested. "What did you see last night?"

"What could I see? I simply couldn't sleep, that's all. And I don't feel much like it tonight."

"You were certainly watching something when I woke up."

"Oh, that. Someone—Thor perhaps—went out. Probably to see that the chickens weren't freezing to death."

He began matter-of-factly to empty his pockets on the dressing table beside her.

Reminded, she looked up. "Dyke, that wooden button. Where is it? Let me have it for Fleur. It may mean a lot to her."

"You didn't tell her about it!"

"No. But she feels so dreadfully about Huldah. And she thinks—hopes, anyway—Huldah may have left something as a sort of message."

"If she did, I didn't see it. Nor Thor before me. Nor Jud LaRue after me. He was one of the men I met on the path this morning."

He looked around. "Where's the coat you were wearing this afternoon?"

"Hanging in that closet. Why?"

He was already opening the door. After a moment he emerged, a half-smile on his lips.

"Dyke, if you don't tell me what you're up to, I'll—"

"Nothing much. But tomorrow, or soon, perhaps, you're going to find in that pocket, or somewhere, the base of the glass I broke in the tavern this afternoon. Don't touch it any more than you can help. Wrap your handkerchief around it and give it to me."

"Why?"

"Because I slipped that glass base into your pocket. And it isn't there now."

"How can you say no with one corner of your mouth and yes with the other?" she flared. "You act as if I were a child, a refugee child who—who can't understand English."

He sat down on the bench beside her, smiled at her in the mirror. "Darling, you not only understand English, but you read a dozen meanings into every word. You're a wonderful wife in New York, but here—you're dynamite."

She was not to be diverted. "You do think Huldah's death was no accident. I know it."

"How can I think or know it? There isn't a single bit of proof to back that up. That sheriff isn't as dumb as he looks. And, if you'll pardon me, neither am I."

When she remained skeptical, he added, "I think something's going on here, certainly. But not what you think. And I'm saying nothing to you or anyone else in this house until I know."

Nan came back from a prolonged study of the darkness to feel Dyke stiffen beside her, then begin cautiously to slide up on his pillow, his hand reaching for the lamp cord.

As its subdued light winked on, she stiffened also. Beulah Bundy, buttoned to the chin in a brown wool robe, her feet deep in purely functional slippers, had stopped halfway toward them from the door.

She ignored Nan to fix her eyes on Dyke while her lips framed one word. "Come."

He swung his feet to the floor and into his slippers as he groped for the sleeves of his robe. Beulah's eyes, tactfully averted, reached the chair in the window, passed over it as if its arrangement meant nothing. Turning, she followed Dyke to the door.

At his gesture, Nan turned off the lamp, sat up, listening tensely. Not a sound, but within heartbeats she knew she was alone.

She remained upright, listening. Now and then the house creaked somewhere, a nail cracked. Gradually she became aware of another sound, low, very near.

It did not come from the hall or from outside the house. By deduction, she traced it to the other side of the wall. Slipping out of bed, she tiptoed over, pressed an ear to the locked door.

In the next room Peggy was weeping as if her heart would break.

When Dyke returned a half-hour later, Nan still sat upright, every light in the room blazing. So were her eyes.

"Hold it," he advised wearily. "I've had about all I can take tonight."

"What happened?"

"Nothing much. Mrs. Devens and Beulah were having an argument about property contracts—things like that. What a house! They think I'm omnipotent."

Between anger and triumph, Nan was practically stymied. "Now I know you're lying, darling. You've been deceiving me all along. From what I saw, Ruby Devens had no interest in this world's property. I must say you and Beulah did a wonderful job of bringing her back. Where did you learn your medical—"

"You followed me!"

"Not right away. But soon enough to know Ruby had tried to poison herself with something in a glass of whisky. What's that in your hand? Phew!" She wrinkled her nose. "Whisky!"

"Don't tell me you don't know!" Dyke had taken a sodden handkerchief from his pocket, held it gingerly as he looked about.

"I suppose you're going to have that analyzed."

"I am." He wrapped the handkerchief in some of her cleansing tissues, then disappeared into the bathroom to scrub his hands. When he came back, he demanded at once, "Where were you? In the corridor?"

"Where else? But just for a minute. Long enough to see—and hear—what was going on?"

"Why didn't you stay? Or come in? We could have used you."

"Because someone else was there."

"In the hall! Who?"

"I don't know. I just felt someone near me—and coming nearer. I got back here in nothing flat."

"No sign of anyone when I came out. And every door was closed."

"It could have been anyone in the house—except Peggy."

"Why leave her out?"

"Because she was crying her eyes out—in there. That's why I got up in the first place. I heard her, went to her door. She wouldn't answer, do anything. Just stopped crying."

"So then you came to Mrs. Devens' room? Through that black corridor!"

"Ruby's door was partly open."

In the act of tossing his bathrobe to the bed, Dyke stopped to look at her anxiously. "I don't know what to do with you, Nan. I asked you not to come to Seattle, I've asked you to go back to New York. And to keep that little nose of yours where it belongs. You're not a child."

"No, I'm not, am I? I'm your wife, Dyke. Oh, darling, don't try to pretend to me that everything's rosy. I know something is terribly wrong. I know you're trying to do something about it. I know you didn't come out here on some case, but to help Fleur. But she's my friend, too, Dyke. And I have a right to know what you know. To do what I can to help her, too."

He studied her thoughtfully. "Look, Nan, I'll make a bargain with you. Wait a few days. Mrs. Devens' attempt to take herself out of this world may be the end of the story. If it is, it won't take me long to click things together. Decide what to do. If it isn't, then I'll tell you what I've learned and you can decide for yourself what you want to do."

"Tell me something now. How did Beulah know to come for you? Fleur says she and Ruby never speak to one another when they're alone."

"Beulah became curious, then suspicious when Mrs. Devens didn't go to bed. She heard her moving around, talking to herself, tearing up papers, doing other odd things for this hour of the night in this house. Finally, alarmed, she came for me. When I barged in, Mrs. Devens was lying on her bed, fully dressed, as you saw, the whisky glass in her hand. Either the sight of me or thought of what she was trying to do terrified her so she couldn't speak. Just gurgle, and drop the glass. She'd already taken a little—fortunately not much. She should be all right after a good night's sleep."

"You seem very sure she won't try again."

"Not tonight, she won't. Beulah's sitting right beside her."

"Dyke! You don't think— Remember how reluctant she was to let us in yesterday, how watchful and uneasy she's been ever since we came? She was terrified, too, tonight in the living room and while the sheriff was here."

"She is terrified. But if you mean she's afraid she may be accused of Huldah's death, don't say it. Don't think it—of her or anyone. That's an order."

"Why?"

"Because the death of Huldah is closed. She died a natural death—by accident."

"What about that button?"

"Huldah didn't toss that button into, the broom patch, my child. If you could find it, don't you think I could? Or Thor? Or the sheriff?"

"You think someone put it there to be found?"

He groaned, crawled in beside her and shut off the light.

"I don't believe that, Dyke. You've forgotten those stains."

"How do you know they were bloodstains? And if blood, human blood. And if human blood, Huldah's specifically."

She thought that over. "I don't, I guess. But Dyke, I know something we can do tomorrow and help Fleur at the same time. And maybe find more buttons. We could go over to Huldah's house at Cranford. We might learn something about David, too. Find the address of a relative. Someone who has a legal right to claim him."

Dyke groaned again and swung his feet to the cold floor. In a moment the blanket from the window chair settled over the bed. "We're going to need this," he told her when she pulled on the light to look at him.

But she knew better. Dyke had seen someone leave the house the night before. Expected someone to leave again, now changed his mind. Why? Because her mention of Huldah's house had suggested to him that that someone had gone there the night before, wouldn't be going back?

Dyke was giving a very good imitation of sound sleep, but she lay, wide-eyed, gazing into the darkness, spinning plans.

If Fleur would do nothing for herself, she'd do something for Fleur. Find someone to claim David. Then she'd take Fleur away. Back to New York, permanently or temporarily. If Fleur left Madrona Place, the Barnacles would have to leave, too. Then Fleur could return—if she wished.

Nan smiled to herself. Perhaps Fleur wouldn't wish? Dyke knew many eligible men.

She sighed, thinking of Huldah. Then deliberately thrust her thoughts aside. Huldah was dead. The case closed. Dyke had said so. Jud LaRue had said so. And she herself had nothing to support that fear she had seen in her own eyes in the compact mirror. Nothing. Not even the button.

21
Wednesday Morning, January 16

Driving with Dyke in Fleur's car to Cranford the next morning, Nan surveyed the world with clearer eyes. Everything was working out. She had not even had to suggest that she and Dyke visit Huldah's cottage. Fleur herself had asked them to go.

Already, under pressure of the housing shortage, letters of inquiry from the two real estate offices in Laketon had arrived in the morning mail. Only lack of telephone connections, apparently, had prevented their calling Monday evening or Tuesday!

With the entire household going into Seattle at three to attend a brief service for Huldah before cremation, Fleur had asked them to go to Cranford, bring back any of Huldah's possessions remaining there, and a report on the condition of the house.

Except that the wind still blew frigidly from the north, the day too was promising. The air was clear of fog. Firs banking the winding highway on both sides made clear green cutouts against the low whitish sky.

Occasionally through a gateway or opening in the trees, she looked across winter-green lawns to comfortable homes set in more greens. A sweet country, even on a winter's day. Breathtaking when skies were blue and sunny and the Olympics and Cascades walled east and west horizons.

"Cranford just ahead, I think," Dyke murmured beside her.

They were running down toward the lake. On the right, roofs of two or three stores rose among trees.

"That's it. Drive straight past the general store. Huldah's house, Fleur said, is half a mile beyond. Second on the right, facing the lake."

Dyke slowed the car to glance at the filling station and general store with post office and barbershop signs posed on either side of its door. And continued slowly to the neat white picket fence with an RFD box before its gate, lettered in clear black, "Huldah Swenson."

"Look here, Nan," he said when he stopped, "let's get something straight right now. You're planning to take a hand in Fleur's affairs, aren't you? I'm sorry to seem to be dictating to you so often, but that's out."

Before she could ask her inevitable why, he told her. "Fleur has too many people trying to direct her life as it is."

"But she's too young, too attractive," Nan protested. "It's ridiculous as well as stupid for her to adopt some other woman's child."

"I agree with you. But that isn't the point. She's entitled to live her life as she wants to live it. Fond of David as she is, she's clinging to him now for another reason. As a sort of symbol of the independence she feels she's losing with that crowd around her. Like you, she can be pushed so far. Then she'll make a stand. And she's been pushed almost to the limit now, I'd say. If you add your weight to the others, she may make that stand on David."

He opened the door beside him as if the matter were settled, then turned back to add, "Fleur needs your support, hon, not opposition or criticism right now. You're the only one she can really turn to. Let her talk to you. Get some of the load off her mind."

Nan's stiffness melted. "I know. But it's for her own good to get David away. That's the only way we can get her to leave Madrona Place."

"Take Fleur away from Madrona Place!"

"Of course. She must leave it, close it up. To force those Barnacles out. If she didn't have David, we could take her with us to New York."

"So that's it." After a moment of thunderstruck silence, Dyke grinned at her. "Find her a husband. Settle her in the next apartment to ours and we'll all live happily, eh? It won't do, Nan, and you should be the first to know it. Fleur's roots are too deep in Madrona Place. You can see in the very way she touches the walls, that newel post, what it means to her. Madrona Place is her true love."

He slid out from under the wheel. "Promise?"

"I won't say any more to Fleur," she agreed. "But that doesn't mean, I'll stop thinking."

She opened her own door to stand beside him and look over the low white fence to the small white house set back on a narrow lawn. One blue spruce stood sentinel beside it. Narrow walks ran round the house on either side. At the rear, on the left, a small white shed circled by chicken netting was a smaller duplicate of the house itself.

Nan shivered. "Let's go in. Get it over."

They moved up the graveled walk to a tiny ground-level porch. Dyke unlocked the door, swung it open. The dead chill of the house rushed out at them. "Perhaps there's wood. I'll light a fire."

But when they stepped into the small square living room, they could see at a glance a fire was unnecessary. Except for framed photographs of Grandfather and Granny Wales, others of Fleur, there was nothing there to be removed.

Inexpensive pine furniture showed an unmarred film of dust, the mirror above the fireplace needed polishing.

Nowhere did they find a letter or personal paper of any kind. If the rest of the house matched this, an hour's cleaning would make it ready for habitation.

The rest of the house did. In the single bedroom only an old sweater hanging from a hook remained of Huldah's personal possessions. Nan gasped as she took it down. It was a mate to the one she had seen in David's arms.

His Oodoo was Huldah! In spite of the old woman's sternness, then, the boy had been attached to her, dependent on her. Now missed her care.

Dyke peered into a tiny bathroom, crossed a short hall to the kitchen. "Nothing here but dishes and the usual pots and pans," he reported. "The house can be rented right now. Just as it stands."

"It's like Huldah," Nan murmured. "She was a sort of pine woman. Just straight and strong, I mean, without branches and leaves and flowers."

"Why don't you wait for me in the car, hon?" Dyke suggested as she shivered. "I'll look around outside, lock up, be right out."

She left gladly, eager to escape the stark little house. At the gate she looked back. Anyone could have lived there; no one could have lived there.

Turning, she bumped into the RFD box. How like Huldah, she thought in some part of her mind, to follow the conventions. Everyone had a mailbox, so she had had to set one up too! Absently, she jiggled the latch, pulled down the door.

At sight of the single letter lying just inside, her eyes focused sharply. She didn't need to pick it up to know that Rensselaer, Struthers, and Bayles, 165 Broadway, New York City, formed the corner card on that familiar rectangle. But she did—to see D.W.H.—Dyke's initials typed above the firm's title. In the righthand corner, an air-mail stamp.

She glanced round. Dyke was nowhere to be seen. No one was in sight on the highway either. Nothing except a small coupé parked in front of the nearest house, a block or two away.

Thrusting the letter into her pocket, she closed the box, hurried back to the car. There a nice point faced her. To whom did the letter belong now? Fleur? Dyke?

Certainly not to Fleur, she decided. If Huldah had asked Dyke to write her at Cranford, she obviously wanted no one at Madrona Place to know of it. If she showed it to Dyke, he would undoubtedly take it over. In either case, she might never learn what it contained. And, curiosity was making X rays of her eyes.

Crunching gravel warned her it was too late, to open the letter here. Dyke was striding down the path toward her, Huldah's sweater over one arm, the photographs in one hand.

Quickly she made a bargain with her conscience. Dyke must know this letter was somewhere. If he looked in that mailbox, she'd give it to him. If he didn't, she'd read it herself.

Dyke didn't even glance at the mailbox. Opening the rear door of the car, he tossed the things onto the seat, hurried round to slide under the wheel, put the car in gear.

"Brrrr! I'm glad that's over. How about food? How about driving in to Seattle for luncheon? We could pick up our bags at the Grandview and mail, if any— Damn!"

He pulled over to the side of the road, shut off the engine. The little coupé Nan had seen parked down the road drew up beside them.

"Hi, folks!" Jud LaRue climbed out, walked over to lean his arms on the window Dyke hastily lowered. He smiled across the wheel at Nan. "I'll take that letter, Mrs. Holliman."

"Letter?" Nan and Dyke chorused.

"Letter. I was interested to see who'd come over to get it." He placed a hand on the wheel, palm up. Flushing a little under Dyke's quizzical gaze, Nan drew the letter from her pocket, placed it in the big brown grasping fingers.

"We've been going through the cottage to pick up Huldah's belongings," he said. "Miss Wales already has renters and buyers—"

"Just mention your home is for sale these days, and twenty-four hours later it's not only sold but the new owners are moving in. This is a real nice little place for someone at that. Too bad Huldah ever left it. She might be alive today if she'd let well enough alone. But then, women never do."

Dyke laughed, but Nan asked coldly, "What do you mean by that?"

"Well, the way I figure it, she'd done about all she could for the Wales family. Had a right to a little rest and life of her own. A small garden, a few chickens, just enough to keep her busy. But what does she do? Goes off somewhere and comes back with David. Oh, he's a cute little tyke, and maybe she was lonely. But that's what I mean. Wasn't any call for her to take on a child."

"Local boy?" Dyke asked.

"Lord, I don't know. I doubt if even Miss Fleur knows. Huldah was awful closemouthed."

He shook his head, shifted his weight. "How's Miss Fleur? Too bad that fool Prentiss kid lost his head, stirred up this mess. Though I guess he wasn't so much to blame, at that. The D.A. comes up for re-election in the spring. This looked like a good chance to get his name in the news, maybe. Hasn't been anything like a real crime around here for years. Chicken stealing's about the worst we have to contend with—outside the shipyard towns in this county. But who'd want to harm—much less kill—an old woman like Huldah? As I told the D.A. 'D.A.,' I says, 'I'd go with you on this if someone else from that house had been found in that broom patch. But the wrong woman's dead.'"

His round blue eyes were fixed on Dyke's face as he talked, bright, like newly washed porcelain.

Dyke asked carefully, "You expected to find someone else in the broom patch?"

"Lord, no! I thought it was much more likely Huldah'd mow down one or all of that bunch of relatives Miss Fleur's got on her hands. Huldah wasn't a woman to take orders. She liked to give 'em. Wouldn't even take 'em from Miss Fleur or old man Wales."

He straightened, spat neatly. "I'll bet plenty of fur flew before those dames got that into their heads. And they all looked like the order-giving kind to me. Maybe that's why none of 'em looked overcome with grief because she's dead. Sounded as if they cared a lot more about saving the Wales name from scandal than about how she died."

Nan's ears caught an angry burr in his rumbling drawl. In fact, as she looked at him now in the clear cold light, he seemed very different from the awkward, embarrassed man who had questioned them so clumsily the night before.

He caught her glance, stepped back. "Well, I'd better let you folks be getting home. Wind's dropping. May get snow." He hesitated, held out the letter to Nan.

"Guess you can have this. The case's closed."

As they drove away, Dyke turned another quizzical eye on his wife. "Next time, young woman, keep your fingers out of booby traps."

"Don't you want this letter?"

"What letter?"

She thrust a finger under the loosely stuck flap, drew out a single sheet of white paper, spread it open. Not a word was written on it.

22
Wednesday Afternoon, January 16

On their return to Madrona Place, they entered a silent house. But the silence held a different quality. Peaceful. Quiet.

Dyke removed the protecting screen from the living-room fire, added logs. "Where is everyone? Another twenty minutes and this fire would be dead."

"Probably dressing, to go into Seattle. It's after one." Nan picked up the things Dyke had dropped on a chair. "I'll put these in Huldah's room, tell Fleur where we're going. That invitation to luncheon, Mr. Holliman, grows on me: I'm starving."

He bowed. "My pleasure, Mrs. Holliman."

She ran up the stairs, smiling to herself at the Hollimans' quaint ways. At the top, paused in surprise. For once the long corridor was neither dim nor dark. Every door standing open permitted light from all the windows to reach it.

In Huldah's doorway she stopped again. She had not seen this room yesterday. Now it had been cleared of any personal possessions, the bed stripped. In the strong white light it reminded her of the little cottage at Cranford. Hastily she dropped sweater and photographs on the table near the door, hurried to her own room.

There, on the dressing table, a note was waiting for her. So hastily scribbled, it was hardly legible:

Nan, dear—sorry you'll find us all gone but Ruby. Thor was able to arrange a one o'clock service and we've had to scramble to make it. Ruby doesn't feel up to going in with us, says she doesn't need anything but sleep. Look in occasionally though, will you? We'll be back as soon as we can. F.

Dropping the note, Nan returned to the corridor, walked back to Mrs. Devens's door. The room was empty as she had thought, the bed made. Pillows, afghans, and other Devensiana seemed normal. And yet there was some difference. She entered the room to look about.

Mirror, comb, and brush from the tortoise-shell set on the dressing table she saw then were missing. And two of the framed Hindu mottoes that had stood on either side of the mirror.

If Ruby had changed her mind, gone in to the service with Fleur, she certainly wouldn't have taken such things with her. But she would if, after Fleur left, she had decided to go to that house in the Magnolia district.

Nan stepped to the closet, opened the door. A crowded rack of dresses and suits on hangers, shelves tightly packed with suitcases and boxes, a floor shelf rowed with small shoes and slippers confronted her. She didn't know Mrs. Devens's wardrobe well enough, however, to know whether anything was missing. Returning to the dressing table, she opened the drawers hesitantly. No sign of the missing toilet-set pieces. No sign of a purse, either.

Turning to leave, she stopped, looked back. Like Fleur, Ruby must have left some word. Not in an obvious place, of course, like a dressing table. Not Ruby!

Impatiently she moved to the bed, tossed back the counterpane. The bed had not been made, merely smoothed over. The nearest pillow still showed a dent and crumpled edge where that small curled head had lain. She picked it up, tossed it aside. Reached, for the other. Nothing there.

But, reaching, her knees struck the bedrail, and something thudded to the floor at her feet. Stooping, she peered at the carpeted floor under the bed.

The heavy brass triangle looked out of place there!

She put out her hand to pick it up, drew back. Hurrying out to the stair well, called Dyke.

He didn't touch the wedge either—at first. Standing back from the bed, he studied the triangle's position carefully. Then moved forward.

"No. I'm too tall. You lie down on the bed, Nan. Place your head in that hollow."

Reluctantly she obeyed.

"Fine. Now drop your right arm over the side, feel with your hand along the bedrail. There. That's right."

Nodding to himself, he picked up the wedge, hefted it in his hand. But all he said was, "Pretty silly of her to venture out on a day like this. After the night she had."

Nan rolled off the bed quickly. "Wouldn't you think she'd have left a note? Fleur did."

He went back with her to their room to read it. "Looks as if that change of hour from four to one didn't leave them much time—they were going to use Thor's car. Perhaps Mrs. D. packed her things and drove in with them. That would explain no note. And Fleur might not have had time to rewrite this one."

"Don't think I'm worrying about little Ruby. It's all right with me if she never comes back."

He placed the note on the dressing table thoughtfully. "See here, you don't look too bright yourself. How about our having something to eat here, taking advantage of everyone's absence to have a quiet afternoon to ourselves? We may not get another chance like this."

"By the fire. Just you and me. Come on. I'll see what there is to eat."

"Ditto. I'll see what there is for a cocktail."

Arm in arm they descended the stairs, Nan for the kitchen, Dyke for the buffet in the dining room. Once, while she was preparing trays, she heard footsteps overhead. But when she opened the foyer door she saw it was only Dyke, entering their room, the brass wedge in his hand.

Happily she returned to her trays. This was going to be nice.

It was. Dyke's daiquiris were always marvelous. And she hadn't done so badly either, thanks to a cold chicken she had found in the icebox. The only trouble was she could hardly keep her eyes open to eat it.

She tried to say that. Perhaps she did. Then her head dropped forward. Dyke rose quickly, rescued her tray and made her comfortable on the couch.

"You need this sleep, Mrs. Holliman," he told her softly.

Placing the screen before the fire, he tiptoed from the room.

Shortly after four, Fleur, with David by the hand, looked in on a peaceful scene: Nan fast asleep on the couch, Dyke asleep in a big chair near by.

As she looked at them, Dyke opened one eye, sat up alertly, tiptoed over. "Thank heaven, you're back. Let her sleep it out, will you? She's all in. And I've got to go in to Seattle."

"Make it snappy then," Thor advised from the open door to the kitchen. "Take Fleur's car. We're in for a storm. Probably snow." He smiled. "While I'm giving orders, I might as well give some more. You follow Nan's and Ruby's example, Fleur, get some rest, too."

"Ruby?" Dyke repeated. "Didn't she go into Seattle with you, Fleur? We thought you hadn't had time to re-write your note."

"Note?" Fleur, stooping to lift David, straightened. "I wrote no note. You mean, Ruby's not here?"

"She was gone when we got back—a little after one."

Thor threw up his hands. Fleur, picking up the drooping David, hurried upstairs. As Dyke started to follow, Beulah spoke his name. Behind Thor in the kitchen, she, Eileen, and Peggy had listened in silence.

Now when Dyke stepped in, she closed the door, burst out, "Drat the woman! But perhaps I'd better go in with you, Dyke. Try to find her. She's in no condition to be out."

Thor vetoed that. "Who's the agent for this house she spoke of? Dyke could see him, find out if she's taken it for a month as she said. Get the address."

No one knew.

"Well, that's out then," he said wearily. "I don't think there's a real estate office in the city she hasn't consulted. She's also followed up advertisements."

"Don't worry about Ruby, Thor." Peggy's young voice was cold. "She does love her comfort, you know. She's probably on her way back right now, thinking about that chicken Beulah baked this morning."

Peggy so seldom spoke that when she did her words had the effect of an oracle.

Snow was already sifting through the still air when Dyke returned at seven. Nan, though awake, still sat drowsily before the fire. From the kitchen came sounds and fragrances of dinner in preparation. And Thor bearing a tray with highball makings.

"Looks like a long hard winter ahead," he greeted Dyke. "The sleeping beauty and I were about to fortify ourselves. Join us?"

Dyke walked over to tousle Nan's hair, drop some letters in her lap. "Feel better, hon?"

She put up her hands and pulled him down by the ears, ostensibly to kiss him. And she did. But she whispered also: "Look. In the fire."

Dyke looked. Thor, coming over with Nan's highball, stopped to smile as Dyke raked something out of the ashes with a poker.

"What's that?"

"Looks like the base of a glass to me," Dyke told him. "What do you make of it?"

"That's good enough for me. Probably came in with the wood."

Thor sighed as he sat down and lifted his glass to Nan. "I'm glad you're here, Nan. And your little boy, too. Maybe, if he's good, David will let him play with his blocks."

"You sound like the old man of the sea," Dyke laughed and, getting up, walked over to mix his own drink. "What's worrying you now?"

"That Devens woman, I suppose. She hasn't returned. Not that I'll lose any weight if she has found a house."

He rose as Fleur and Eileen joined them then. Before he had finished serving their highballs, Peggy appeared.

As they sat about the fire, silent, tired, but relieved too, Nan looked admiringly at the three Wales women. In spite of their differences in ages, backgrounds, and personalities, they were all unmistakably Wales. Only Peggy had authentic beauty, but Fleur had a lovely poise and, when she wasn't troubled, graciousness. Eileen had that elusive charm. Beulah, too—well, there was something striking about Beulah, she conceded.

She was amusing herself, finding comparisons for their black Wales eyes when she discovered they had one quality in common. Fleur's, in their velvety softness, might suggest black pansies. Eileen's, at the moment, at least, might suggest night—the high, mysterious night sky over New York in July. Peggy's—pools of clear, still water, so deep they appeared black. Beulah's—sharp, ebony-pointed gimlets. But they were all unreadable. You looked at their eyes, not into them.

Absorbed, she hadn't listened to the desultory conversation about her. Now Thor's worried voice recalled her. He stood, peering through curtains at the falling snow.

"It's almost eight. If Ruby's coming, she'd better come soon. This storm is really something."

"Let's wait till eight," Fleur suggested. "If she's not here then, we won't wait any longer. The snow may make the busses late."

"Sure she didn't leave a note?"

"There's nothing. Peggy looked, too."

Dyke rose. "Anyone look at that note Nan found? Could Ruby have written it herself?"

But that note was never found. When the search for it was abandoned, Peggy again visited Mrs. Devens's room, returned to announce,

"She isn't coming back. Her small black bag's gone and some things from her dressing table. A couple of dresses, too."

"Wouldn't she take more than that if she intended to be gone a month?" Nan asked.

"I know one thing," Thor declared. "If we don't hear from her tomorrow, I'm reporting her missing to Jud LaRue. We've had one lesson."

Into the startled silence Beulah's deep voice bloomed: "You'd better come to dinner—if you want to see it. The lights are flickering. Looks to me as if they won't last much longer."

As soon as they reached the dining room, Thor turned on the radio. The storm, a voice was reporting, was sweeping the Northwest, as far south as Portland, as far north as Alaska. The forecast was for continued snow and cold.

To flickering lights, reports, and dinner progressed. Cars and busses on hill lines in Seattle were already stopping, blocked by snow and slippery streets. Hundreds of people, unable to return home, were crowding the hotels. . . . Bus lines out of the city might not be able to continue after midnight. . . . School children were advised to keep in touch with the radio. If the storm continued all night, schools might have to be closed. . . .

The lights flared up brightly, went out. The radio died.

"Snowbound!" Peggy said. "Twentieth-century version. Yet it's still like a poem, isn't it?"

While Fleur found candles, the others wandered from window to window watching the shadowy white mass flow steadily, silently down. Like a solid curtain, Nan thought, shutting them off from the world.

The room was warm, but unaccountably she shivered, remembering.

"Wait," Dyke had said. "Mrs. Devens' attempt to take herself out of this world may be the end of the story."

But—if she had tried again! What if she were out in that darkness—that whiteness—now?

She was trying to reassure herself with thought of that little black bag when Fleur exclaimed behind her, "Thor, where are you going?"

Turning, she saw Fleur's eyes, wide and anxious above the flames of two tall candles in her hands. Following her gaze, Nan found Thor at the porch door, pulling on a coat. He picked up a large flashlight from the window sill before he answered:

"Down the woods path."

23
Sunday Morning, January 20

Through Thursday, Friday, and Saturday the storm continued, working up to the fury of a midwestern blizzard. Dense, fine snow, driven by a shrieking wind, fell solidly, heavily, as if it had become a permanent feature of the landscape.

A phenomenon unrecorded for more than a quarter-century on Puget Sound. To overcrowded and unprepared Seattle and the surrounding area, it was more than that. It was complete paralysis.

Stores, offices, schools, churches, industries, war plants, everything closed their doors. All forms of transportation stopped. Telephone, telegraph, and electric lines went down under wind and snow. Thousands were marooned in hotels, farmhouses, ranches. Hundreds of thousands more were equally marooned in their homes, as isolated from the world as if they had been set down on the most remote inlet of Hudson Bay.

When at last it quieted toward midnight on Saturday, blew itself out with Sunday's dawn, cities, towns, villages, fields, highways smothered under four to eight feet of snow.

At Madrona Place the sun, bursting through routed clouds in midmorning of Sunday, made a blinding brilliance of a strange, white, motionless, and silent world.

163

And, with the exception of David, the eight people inside the snowbanked and -blinded house were almost as silent and motionless.

That mental and physical inertia had not come on them suddenly, but inevitably through the long days, while they tried to speed the creeping hours. The silence that had greeted Thor's return on Wednesday midnight had set the pattern. Again and again, and for longer periods it had returned.

Reading, playing games, talking about the fire, preparing, and eating meals, feeding the fires, finding a thousand small tasks to be done, they had fought it. Particularly with David they had fought it. But inexorably when he returned to the nursery for naps or bed, that silence returned.

Thor had found no trace of Ruby Devens on the woods path. No word of her in Laketon. And since his return, no one had mentioned her. Yet her broad little shadow moved everywhere with everyone much more vividly than her living presence had ever done.

The first rays of the sun struck blue and gold and ruby sparks from the frost and snow on the dining-room windows. Deflected, they entered the room to dance over glassware and mirrors and shining wood surfaces.

The group seated about the late breakfast table watched them dully, hardly comprehending. Then Thor stirred, looked at Dyke.

"Want to try it? Won't be anyone at Wales Center, but if the snow's packed we can reach Laketon."

Nan, with a clamoring David beside her at a window, watched them go. Plunging through waist-deep snow to the back road, they crossed it for the woods path. Fine snow flew up in clouds as they floundered along, disappearing occasionally as one or the other fell. The sight filled David with glee, Nan with anxiety. They looked so small, yet so grim in that unbroken expanse of scintillating white.

She was relieved when Fleur called from the kitchen. Robins, Alaskan robins, flickers, blue jays, a host of smaller birds were pouring out of the sky in flocks into the west orchard. Their cries filled the air as they swooped about the apple trees where frozen apples offered food after their long abstinence. David deserted Nan with alacrity to watch them.

Returning to her dining-room window, Nan found she had a fellow watcher. Peggy stood there, frowning against the sun, her fine lips a straight angry line.

Long, cold blue shadows were stretching across the snowy lawns of late afternoon when Dyke and Thor returned. Breathless, exhausted, half frozen.

No telephone message had been received from Mrs. Devens at Laketon.

"You should know better, than to expect one," Beulah scolded. "She thinks only of herself, that one. But take my word for it, she'll be back. I can't see her living alone, doing anything for herself, when she can have everything done for her here."

Beulah's way of whistling to keep up her courage!

"Did you call Jud LaRue?" Fleur asked.

Thor nodded. "He doesn't think much can be done tonight. Not much chance of anything opening before noon tomorrow. But he says if Ruby reached Seattle, we've no reason to worry. No casualties reported there. He didn't have much time to talk. He's swamped with calls and telegrams from all parts of the county asking for relatives and friends who haven't shown up at home."

Having taken some action, Thor's spirits rose. As he and Dyke thawed out, they retailed news of the storm they had picked up in the village.

Madrona Place hadn't done so badly after all. At least they'd had heat, an oil range for cooking and hot water. The Lake district, almost entirely dependent on electricity, had been thrown back to the days of the Pilgrim Fathers when the current ceased to flow.

"Look!" Peggy turned excitedly from the radio. "The current's on now!" She sped for a light switch. It responded, too.

They gazed at the glowing lamps, listened to a toothy old voice in a radio commercial urge everyone on a pension to hurry to Montgomery's Dental Clinic for a free examination as if they were the first people in all history to see and hear such wonders.

Suddenly they became gay, almost hysterically so, laughing at everything and nothing, as together they prepared dinner. The evening winked by.

At midnight Fleur tentatively suggested bed.

Peggy, sitting on the floor beside Thor, her face flushed and lovely in the firelight, protested. "Oh, not yet. I wish we could go on like this—forever."

She bit her lips. Then abruptly rose and vanished by way of the back stairs. Thor remained impassive, his kind blue eyes veiled.

Cold returned with renewed vigor on Monday. Except for an occasional giant truck breaking a trail through the solid snow of the highway, the continuous murmur of the radio—left on for bulletins concerning the shipyards— Madrona Place was again isolated.

Though the storm had ended and tension over Ruby's absence relaxed, another crisis appeared to be brewing. Thor joined the family only for meals, ate silently, returned to his workshop in the basement. Occasionally Dyke went down to help him with something that sent a dry, rasping rumble through kitchen and dining room.

Peggy, barricaded behind a book in one corner of the dining room, looked unseeingly for minutes at a time at any page to which it opened. Only when Thor appeared did she come to life.

Fleur remained with David most of the time in the nursery. He had caught a slight cold, she said.

Alternately amused and irritated, Nan looked on, unable to decide whether it was Thor's wishes or Fleur's the girl seemed determined to challenge.

Only Eileen and Beulah, true Wales, went their own way. Eileen making sketches of the well, now a miniature pyramid of dazzling jewels, of every snow-laden tree and bush, of every view from every window. Beulah concocting strange and wonderful dishes in the kitchen.

When at last, Monday evening, the radio announced that the Lake Washington Shipyards would open at seven Tuesday morning, a soundless sigh of relief went up from everyone. A later announcement that all bus lines out of Seattle would resume operation Tuesday noon brought audible relief from Dyke.

"Thank heaven!" he said to Fleur. "Theoretically I'm here to work, you know."

"We've all been under a strain for so long!" Relief echoed in her voice, too. "I'm sorry you and Nan had to share it. But we'll be back to normal in a day or two now. You'll see."

She was right. Tuesday morning before seven Thor and Peggy went down to the crossroads to meet their share-the-ride car. Like the doves from the Ark, they did not return. Dyke caught the first bus for Seattle that crept along the highway at noon.

And Fleur, Beulah, and Nan spent the day moving Ruby's things into Huldah's room, Peggy's into Ruby's, and restoring the sitting room of the guest suite to its original role.

Nan worked busily, while her romantic head wove plans. It would be nice for her and Dyke to share a sitting room of their own. It would also be nice for Peggy and Thor! After all, she rationalized, Peggy deserved some compensation.

Wednesday was even more normal. Under a sun blazing down from a clear blue sky, the snow was settling and melting rapidly. Even the Cascades were visible, gloriously white under crowns of new snow. Traffic filled the highway, though no mailman as yet had ventured up the snowbound dirt road.

That evening, however, Dyke returned from Seattle with a letter over which he and Beulah talked some time in the Hollimans' sitting room. Talked so long that Fleur and Nan were left to see that dinner reached the table.

Hardly had they succeeded and the family been collected from all parts of the house when the screen door to the back porch slammed sharply. Heavy footsteps stamped across the porch. Remembering another evening when they had sat at this table listening to running footsteps cross that porch, no one moved for a moment. Then Thor rose and opened the house door. Jud LaRue stood just outside.

This time there was no embarrassment in his manner or apology for his inopportune arrival. He walked straight to the table to look from face to face.

"I haven't found your Mrs. Devens," he said then. "But I've had word of her. As of a week ago Tuesday."

"Isn't that the day she found the house in Magnolia?" Dyke asked. "We saw her after that, Sheriff. You did too, at this table."

"I don't know about any house. Doubt if there is one." The sheriff's drawl was flat, assured. "Didn't you folks know she's been working two days a week—since last June—in a bakery? Out near the university."

Incredulity answered him.

"Well, she has." He sat down then in the chair Thor had placed for him, went right on. "How do I know? I ran her name in the Monday evening papers in a list of people our office had inquiries about due to the storm. This afternoon Waller Beumeister showed up."

"Who's Beumeister?" Thor wanted to know.

"The fellow who owns the bakery. He's a Dutchman and he's plenty mad. It seems he's been paying her fifteen dollars for the two days. And Tuesday—the fifteenth, I mean—when she was leaving, she asked him to advance her twenty-five dollars. She'd been almost a dead loss all day, so he knew she was in some sort of trouble. But he let her have it. Was afraid he'd lose her if he didn't. Well, that's the last he saw of Mrs. Devens and his money."

24

Wednesday Evening, January 23

Beulah and Dyke exchanged glances. Dyke leaned forward.

"Mrs. Bundy and I," he told the sheriff, "have been keeping something from Miss Wales—everyone here. We didn't want to speak until we knew. Now we do. We were going to tell the family tonight; then, if they thought I should, I was going to call on you tomorrow."

He took a letter from an inside pocket, but didn't open it. "Naturally everyone in this house was distressed over the discovery of Huldah's body in the broom patch Monday night. Mrs. Devens, too. Yet she went into Seattle Tuesday morning as usual and that evening when she returned told of this little house she had found at last. . . .

"Shortly after she had told us, you arrived, Sheriff. As you noticed, perhaps, she was very nervous, frightened by all your questions. When you left she went up to her room, apparently to pack a bag to take in to Seattle, planning to spend a month there. Instead, as Mrs. Bundy will tell you, she spent the evening destroying papers. Finally, alarmed, Mrs. Bundy came for me."

In the deepening silence he told then of Mrs. Devens's attempt to take her life, of his and Beulah's role in frustrating it.

"She denied it," he concluded. "Swore she had merely been taking a sleeping tablet with the whisky to make

sure of a good night's sleep. She was right as far as she
went. But she dropped the glass when I entered the room.
I wiped up the whisky with a handkerchief and Wednesday
took it to a chemist. This afternoons I received his report.
He found that Mrs. Devens had dissolved enough veronal
in that one glass to kill several people."

"Oh, Beulah, why didn't you come for me?" Fleur asked,
shocked. "Have told me, at least. That was why she was ill
Wednesday morning. We should never have left her alone."

"Ill!" Beulah snorted. "Ill enough to get up and walk
out of this house without leaving a word to say where she
was going."

"Perhaps she did go to that house," Nan suggested.
"Maybe that twenty-five dollars she borrowed was for
rent—"

"I doubt it," LaRue interrupted. "I've checked with a
number of agencies—all the important ones that handle
property in the Magnolia district. None of them had her
name on their lists. No one remembered ever talking with
her."

He paused, said significantly, "It struck me that Tuesday night I was here she was more than upset. She looked
like a scared rabbit to me. She was the only one who didn't
say a word."

"She was terrified," Dyke told him.

"That's what I said," the sheriff told him. He turned to
Fleur. "Can you remember what you all did, Miss Fleur?
Wednesday morning."

"If the others will help me. That's a complicated request. Thor went in to Seattle shortly after eight. Peggy
walked down to Wales Center about nine-thirty to wait
for his telephone call. He said then he'd arranged a service
for Huldah for four o'clock that afternoon. That gave us
loads of time, of course, so we didn't do anything about
getting ready. Oh yes, the mail came, with inquiries about

Huldah's house at Cranford. About eleven or so the Holli-mans went over to see what it needed."

She talked slowly, waiting for nods of verification from the others.

"They'd been gone only a few minutes when a boy came running up from Wales Center with a message. Thor had been able to get the crematory chapel for one o'clock instead of four. Thinking that would be better, he'd signed up for that time. That gave us only an hour or so to do everything. Beulah and Eileen didn't wait for me. They went in on the first bus they could catch to get flowers—"

"I caught the eleven-thirty bus from Laketon," Beulah corrected. "Eileen took the next one—at noon—from the crossroads. We didn't go in together."

"Peggy wrestled with Thor's car while I dressed David," Fleur said then. "When we were ready I took him out to the garage, warmed up the car while Peggy dressed. We were a little late in getting started. It was after half past twelve when Peg came out."

"Then you were the last to see Mrs. Devens?" the sheriff asked. "She was still in bed?"

Peggy shook her head. "I never went near her. I didn't even know she was ill. Really ill, I mean. She could always manage a headache when she wanted to get out of something."

"Those were my sentiments, too," Eileen said.

"I took her some coffee about nine," Fleur told LaRue. "She said to take it away, she wanted to sleep." Her lips straightened. "What she actually said was that since she'd seen entirely too much of Huldah alive, she had no desire to see her—dead. I—well, I didn't go back. I didn't realize she was ill—"

"Then I must have been the last one," Beulah interrupted. "I looked in just before ten. I don't think she was sleeping, but she pretended to be. That didn't sit well with me, since I'd been up most of the night with her. I didn't go back."

"What time did you get back here?" Without comment LaRue turned his blue eyes on Dyke.

"A little after one."

"So—she left here then between half past twelve and one? Pretty quick work to get up and dress and down to the crossroads—"

"Not necessarily," Thor said. "She could have left any time after Beulah saw her. No trick at all to go down the back stairs to the basement. Not one chance in a thousand of anyone seeing her leave that way. There isn't a single window in the back of the house upstairs."

"And after ten no one was in either the kitchen or dining room," Beulah assured him.

"You saying she might have taken the woods path to Laketon?" the sheriff drawled, a curious note in his rumble.

"If she did, Jud, *she went all the way,*" Thor spoke quickly. "I went over every inch of that path and the broom patch too, Wednesday night."

The sheriff took up Thor's fork, poked thoughtfully at the tablecloth with it. Beulah's gimlet eyes bored into him without effect.

"Perhaps I pulled a boner the first time I was here, Miss Fleur," he said finally. "I said the death of Huldah Swenson was a closed case so far as my office was concerned. And the D.A. agreed with me. It was—we didn't have a mite of evidence to prove she hadn't died of a heart spasm resulting from her fall and struggles in that broom patch. Now I'm not so sure! From what you said I gather Mrs. Devens had no love for Huldah Swenson. Think she had any reason to hate or fear her? Hate or fear her enough to want her out of the way?"

A wave of emotion rose from the table, hung almost tangibly in the air.

After a time Thor said, "Huldah was a tall, strong woman in spite of her age. Ruby not much over five feet. Not very strong, either."

"She wouldn't need to be," the sheriff said calmly. "Let's suppose something like this: Huldah leaves the house early that Saturday morning. It's dark until after eight this time of year. Mrs. Devens follows her, catches up with her on that path. It was slippery, remember. Just a good push would be enough to throw Huldah off balance, send her falling. Or there was that apple branch, remember? She could have tripped her."

He looked around. No one was willing to suppose with him.

A deeper rumble came into his drawl. "I'm just supposing, remember, but maybe we're getting somewhere. Huldah had received a blow on the head. If she was lying on the ground from a fall, a child could have struck her, or a woman a foot shorter. Struck her hard enough to knock her unconscious, but not kill her."

Perhaps the horror-ridden silence moved him to lift his head. His eyes more opaque than ever, he looked round, paused on Dyke. Dyke also looked as if he had received a blow.

"That all you had on your mind, Mr. Holliman? Just that letter? I'll take it along, please."

Dyke passed the letter down the table before he answered. "No. No, perhaps I have something else. If you'll, excuse me a moment, I'll get it."

No one moved or spoke in the minute or two he was gone. When he returned he carried the brass wedge in his hand. Without a word he placed it before the sheriff.

A shadow drew down over LaRue's dark face. He hunched forward to look at the triangle with such concentration that his black brows formed one straight line across his face. His thick lips pursed in a soundless whistle when finally he picked it up, hefted it as Dyke had done. "Where'd you get this?"

Dyke told him.

"You think it might have been used as a weapon?"

"I don't know that it *had* been used as a weapon," Dyke qualified. "When I discovered where it had fallen from, I thought perhaps it was intended to be used as one. Sounds incredible, but that's the way it looked. It had fallen from the bedrail just about where the right hand of a woman the size of Mrs. Devens could reach it quickly. I tried out my hunch on my wife. Her fingers stopped just two or three inches beyond the place from which the wedge fell. Nan's just about that much taller than Mrs. Devens."

"Brother," the sheriff said solemnly, "now I know we've got something."

"But—that's impossible," Fleur protested. "That desk piece belonged to Ruby. She had every right to have it in her own room if she wanted to. But she didn't. Oh, Dyke, excuse me! I mean I moved that wedge to a bookcase in the living room last Tuesday night for some reason. Oh, I know—Thor wanted the little table it was on for highballs."

"And I placed it back on the table," Nan said quickly. "But—later—the lights went out. When they came on, that wedge was gone!"

Fleur's eyes turned on Beulah. So did everyone's, the sheriff's last of all. They witnessed a miracle.

Slow dark color welled up from Beulah's thin throat, spread in a dark stain to the roots of her hair.

25
Wednesday Evening, January 23

"I never touched it," she said hoarsely. "I do turn out those lights when I think they're being wasted. But I didn't touch them Tuesday night. I knew the Hollimans were in the living room. I—I washed the dishes, then went right to my room by the back stairs. I never went near the front of the house."

"No one has said you did, Beulah," Thor said quietly.

She sat back with a jerk; her corded hands, clenched on the table, fell to her lap.

"Tuesday evening?" Eileen was following some devious route of her own. "Huldah had been dead four days then. Ruby had no reason to fear her."

"She was afraid of Huldah, then?" The sheriff caught her up quickly. "Why?"

"We all were, Sheriff. I told you that before."

"What do you say, Miss Fleur?" he asked then.

Fleur was silent a long time, the fingers of her right hand slowly turning her water glass, her head bent forward. At last she said, "I'd rather not answer that question, Jud, if you don't mind."

"What I want's got nothing to do with it, Miss Fleur."

Her eyes, soft and luminous now with held-back tears, turned on Dyke. "Must I?"

"The sheriff is only doing what he has to do. If you don't answer him here, he'll have to find other—perhaps more unpleasant—ways of learning the truth."

She drew a long breath. "Yes, Ruby hated Huldah," she admitted. "But Huldah hated her, too. Resented her bringing all her furniture."

The sheriff said patiently, "We're talking about why Mrs. Devens hated Huldah."

"To Mrs. Devens, Huldah was a servant. She didn't understand—about Huldah. When Ruby first came she—she gave orders. Huldah ignored her. She didn't like that."

"Why did she hate Huldah enough to want her dead?"

"I don't know that she did," Fleur cried. "You can't prove she did."

The sheriff sat back, looking at her steadily. "Not right away, maybe. But I can tell you this, Miss Fleur. One hour after I leave here I'm going to telephone you— No, I can't do that. Tomorrow morning, then, I'll bring you proof that someone from this house struck Huldah with this brass wedge—"

"Jud!"

Thor turned his head slowly. "Go on, Sheriff. If you can prove that, I want to know it. I owe a lot to Huldah I've never had a chance to pay back."

"Yeah, I know, Thor." He picked up the wedge, ran a finger along one of its three sharp edges. "We have photographs and measurements of that wound on Huldah's forehead. A deep, narrow wound, like a bad bruise, with a sharp cut right through the center of it. Exactly the kind of wound this brass triangle would make."

Fleur's face appeared to grow smaller, her eyes larger, darker, as she faced him. "You mean—if you can prove that wedge struck Huldah—it was murder?"

LaRue nodded. "I can see how you'd hate to think anyone in this house would kill another, Miss Fleur, but you owe a lot to Huldah, too."

Her eyes moved despairingly round the table. No one spoke. Her resistance collapsed.

"I—I can't believe it. And perhaps what I know isn't enough."

"Let the sheriff decide that," Dyke urged.

"Two weeks ago Ruby made an issue of Huldah," she admitted then. "Over nothing really. Huldah'd thrown out something Ruby had spent all morning cooking. She demanded that I send Huldah away. I refused. Then Huldah was angry. She said I must decide between them. Either Ruby left this house—or she would. I tried to talk her out of it. But she wouldn't listen, So—so I told Ruby she'd have to be the one to go."

"What day was that?" Jud asked.

"Thursday—the Thursday before Huldah went away. That was why—one reason why she wanted to go back to Cranford. She wouldn't stay in the house with Ruby. She said she'd come back when Ruby had gone."

"Anyone else know about this?"

"We all did," Beulah informed him. "The whole house rang with their nonsense. A war going on—men fighting and dying—and Madrona Place is torn apart by a squabble between two women!"

"Squabble is hardly the word," Eileen commented. "Ruby, a Wales, forced to bite the dust at the insistence of a member of the lower clawsses!"

The sheriff doubled one hand to rub his head behind an ear. "What was Mrs. Devens' racket?" he asked in bewilderment. "All this talk about her buying a house, even that she'd found one. Yet the thing she was set on was to stay right here—"

Eileen smiled coolly. "Leave us our little, illusions, Mr. LaRue. We all have them. Mrs. Devens remained here only temporarily while she looked for a new home in Seattle. Mrs. Bundy remains here because one day she hopes to play a strategic role in winning the war. Peggy also

remains"—she cocked a crooked eyebrow at the girl's brim-
ming anger—"for patriotic reasons. And I—I pretend I'm
stuck here because I can't get back to my home in South
Africa. I have no home in South Africa."

LaRue blinked, turned back to Fleur. "In the end, Mrs.
Devens won, didn't she? After Huldah's death you said no
more about her having to leave Madrona Place?"

"No. I said nothing more."

"Just one question more, then. The way I see it, Mrs.
Devens had two grudges against Huldah. One, because of
Huldah she was going to lose her home at Madrona Place.
Two, because of Huldah she'd lost plenty face. Huldah'd
ignored her when she tried to give orders. And when it
came to a showdown, Miss Fleur chose Huldah instead of
her. Now then, you all knew Mrs. Devens. I didn't. Think
she had enough venom in her and enough—guts to follow
Huldah out of this house on a dark morning, try to kill
her?"

He looked at Thor first.

"She was sly, secretive—a pain in the neck generally."
Thor shook his head. "But I can't see her killing anyone—
or trying to."

LaRue turned to Eileen.

She, too, shook her head. "A congenital doormat."

For once he understood her, reported, "Plenty of
people have broken their necks tripping over doormats."

"Oh, if you put it that way, yes."

The blue eyes moved next to Peggy.

Her long eyelids lifted slowly. "I don't know, Mr.
LaRue. She was a nasty, prying weasel of a woman. I don't
think I ought to answer a question like that. I—I don't
know enough about people."

The sheriff's glance crossed the table to Beulah.

Cords in her long, thin neck tightened. "Ruby was
the kind—to inspire others to murder. Stuffed with false

pride. She went out of her way to have it hurt. And to hurt others. I don't know—if she were hurt in a big way, she might try to hurt back—the same way."

LaRue waited for her to say more, but she was silent. He looked then at Nan and Dyke. "We pass," Dyke said for both of them.

Last of all, Jud looked at Fleur. Her eyes, dilated till they showed no white, fixed on his face a long moment. Then slowly her hands moved to her throat, hesitated over the loop of the soft black scarf knotted about it.

With a swift motion she ripped it free. Faint, but still visible, on either side of her white neck were blue-gray bruises.

"Yes, she could try to kill. She tried to kill me."

26
Wednesday Night, January 23

How blind they had been! How blind not to read in Ruby's strange conduct signs of a desperate, terrified woman attempting to escape the nemesis of her own thoughts and acts!

Nan stood at the front window of the bedroom, looking out at the quiet white night. But not seeing it. Through her mind poured the flood of substantiating detail that had followed Fleur's dramatic revelation.

Bundled in sweaters, Ruby had entered her improvised chapel in that very bedroom the Saturday morning Huldah left the house. Here, the door locked, her lips locked, she had remained, only emerging in the late afternoon for food. Returning, she had even slept here between the rigors of her meditations.

Until that Saturday she had spent an hour or so a day at these devotions, but never before had she gone into a retreat so prolonged!

The arrival of Nan and Dyke, requiring her to remove her meditational properties that they might have a bed, she had resented as crass interference with the unfoldment of her spiritual life.

According to their temperaments, the family had been impatient, irked, amused, or indifferent. Now, too late, they saw in that three-day withdrawal, in every word and

act of Ruby's since that Saturday morning, manifestations
of hidden guilt.

While Jud LaRue listened stolidly, they had gone back
over the past six months. Pointed up Ruby's effrontery in
arriving with vans of furniture that now packed barn and
garage, overflowed in the living room. . . . Ruby's tenacity
in remaining in the face of openly expressed or implied
disinterest in her presence. . . . Ruby's sustained deceit in
working two days a week in that bakery, yet returning each
evening with elaborate accounts of her house-hunting. . . .
Everything added up to a woman capable of any act.

Nan's *they* did not include Fleur. While Jud remained,
Fleur had sat in stricken silence, crushed by the tragedy
that had fallen on Madrona Place. Then she had slipped
away, wordlessly, to her room.

Nan's heart ached for her now. She was the only one
perhaps who could fully understand what Fleur suffered to
see such misfortune descend on this domain Grandfather
Wales had created for an untarnished future. For Fleur to
have been forced to play a part in exposing that misfortune must be the final humiliation.

Resolutely Nan left the window for the sitting room,
where Dyke sat at a table, ostensibly studying a sheaf of
papers before him. She was not deceived. He, too, was
shaken by the events of the evening.

When he didn't look up, she sat down beside him.
"So—the story didn't end with Ruby's attempt to kill herself. And I've waited more than a few days—"

He took off his glasses, rubbed a hand across his eyes,
shook his head. "I never dreamed of this, Nan. I still can't
believe it. I've been working on something entirely different."

"I don't care what you're working on," she retorted.
"Fleur's in trouble, awful trouble. We've both got to help

her. And I can't if I don't know what's at the bottom of all this. It's more than just a fight over whether Ruby stayed or didn't stay, isn't it? She must have had some reason for moving in with all her furniture, sticking it out when she knew no one wanted her."

"So you've thought of that, have you? Then Jud will think of it, too, soon."

"I don't care what Jud thinks."

"You will," he. assured her wearily. "All right. I'll tell you. I wish now I'd told you before. It would have been simpler. But I didn't know when I left New York that anyone other than myself—my mother, rather—was concerned."

"Your mother!"

"Wait. I'll go back. Remember my telling you I didn't know till J.W. died that he had a daughter? He mentioned that in his will, merely to explain why he was leaving everything he owned to my mother. His daughter, Fleur Wales, he said, would be fully provided for by her grandfather."

"You didn't tell me that part of it."

"No," he agreed grimly, "I didn't. Because James Wardman Wales left nothing to my mother. Though he thought he had. From the time he married and moved to Seattle, he had given or sent money to Grandfather Wales to be invested in Madrona Place. Before he died he'd invested a total of more than fifteen thousand dollars."

James Wardman Wales, too! Just as Eileen's and Peggy's fathers, Ruby's husband, Beulah herself had done!

"Naturally my mother wrote at once to Grandfather Wales, enclosing a copy of the will. She received a very simple, friendly reply from him, written and signed by Huldah. It made no direct reference to my stepfather's money. But said, apropos of nothing at all, that Madrona Place had fallen on hard days. Fruit production on a

commercial scale had had to be abandoned, owing to growing competition from eastern Washington orchards. There
was a postscript, explaining that Huldah wrote for him
because his hands were crippled with arthritis." Dyke
turned to his brief case. "I have a copy of that letter here
if you want to read it."

"Not now. Go on."

"That letter was a blow to Mother and to me. Not that
I wanted anything from my stepfather, but I did want my
mother comfortable and I did want to study law. Mother
took the letter to a lawyer, and he very shortly advised
her to make no claims. He'd learned that Madrona Place,
as Huldah had written, was practically valueless. So my
mother took 'paying guests' into our home, and I worked
my way through Yale. And that was that, apparently. Until
Fleur came East. She didn't come as a poor man's grand-
child, you remember."

"No," Nan admitted, remembering Fleur's ample allow-
ance, "she didn't."

"I was graduated by that time, admitted to the New
York bar, but hanging by my teeth to the doorstep of Rensselaer, Struthers, and Bayles. So I wrote to Grandfather
Wales myself. And I also received a letter from him, via
Huldah. A very nice letter. Madrona Place was working out
of its doldrums; Grandfather Wales had great hopes for its
future, etc., etc. That time I checked myself with Fleur.
And I spoke to her about J.W.'s money. She wasn't very
receptive—because, and I don't blame her, she resented his
resenting her. But she did write Huldah. Huldah replied
that J.W. had occasionally sent money for Fleur's support!
And I believe he did. But this fifteen thousand was definitely a business transaction between him and his father.
The wording of the will leaves no doubt about that."

"But Dyke, as you said yourself, there must be records,
receipts—"

"That's what you think! Letters, yes. Personal letters, though written by Huldah, thanking him for this check or that, but never mentioning amounts, dates, or purpose. Nothing that gave any proof—legal proof—that the checks J.W. sent were to be invested in Madrona Place as a business transaction between him and his father. J.W. was too dutiful a son to demand things like receipts!"

"But Grandfather Wales—why, Dyke, he was integrity itself. He wouldn't—he couldn't deliberately do anything like that. Cheat anyone, especially his own son."

She paused, added, horrified, "His own sons. His own sister. And Paul Devens, I don't know exactly what relationship—"

"Nephew. But don't go too fast. We're talking about J.W.—and me. And leave Grandfather Wales out of this for the present, too. Apparently Huldah handled all his business affairs as well as his correspondence."

"You believe Huldah—!"

"Let's jump to January 10. That afternoon I received an air-mail from her—from a very alarmed Huldah. She asked me, begged me, to come to Seattle at once, by plane, if possible. It was an almost incoherent letter, hastily written, as if she wrote with a watchful eye over one shoulder. She said I was the only one who could save Madrona Place from disaster. That she would meet me at the Grandview with all the proofs and information I needed—"

"Dyke! That was practically admitting, wasn't it, that you had a right to act for Madrona Place?"

"That possibility is what brought me out here. I wasn't particularly concerned about relieving Huldah's mind. Well, we arrived. No Huldah at the Grandview. No word of her. No way of reaching her at Madrona Place or at Cranford, where she'd asked me to write or telegraph her. I'd done both. And from the Grandview I called every hotel and rooming house—or would have if you hadn't burst into flame."

Before she could more than gasp at the memory of those hours in the Grandview lobby, he went on:

"Thanks to you, we arrived at Madrona Place. To find representatives of every branch of the Wales clan in possession. But it never occurred to me until that evening, when I talked with Fleur, that they might be victims of the same exploitation J.W. experienced. What Ruby told me the next morning on the bus and Eileen told you seemed to support my hunch."

"You believe Eileen—?"

"What I couldn't understand—don't yet—is how or why they all knew to come here—months ago. Fleur couldn't explain their presence. Their own reasons for being here were pretty flimsy. It could only have been Huldah—"

"That doesn't make sense, Dyke. If Huldah sent for them, why were they all against her? Remember, I thought, after hearing Eileen talk about her father's investments in land, Beulah's and the others—that they were all here to work against Fleur? I still think that. Maybe they have money due them legally from Madrona Place. Maybe they haven't. But they must have learned how valuable this land is, have come to get something out of it—"

When Dyke shook his head, she leaned forward urgently. "Don't you see? That's what Huldah meant by disaster! She'd discover pretty quickly what they were up to. That's why she sent for you. To help stop them."

"And Ruby found out what she was up to? Stopped her? Is that your idea?"

"Ruby was always slipping around, listening, watching—" She broke off to look at him closely. "What did you mean?"

"It could have been Ruby who stopped Huldah, if there's anything in your theory. Or it could have been any of them. Eileen, Beulah, Peggy had the same motive, opportunity. And access to that brass wedge."

"Dyke!" Nan was on fire again. "It couldn't have been just to stop Huldah's reaching you that Ruby took that wedge. It was to get the information and proof Huldah was taking to you. And nothing was found on Huldah, was it? Ruby must have succeeded!"

He shook his head. "I'd say Huldah was too smart for that. She'd never seen me, remember. I may have been her last hope, but even so, she'd have made sure she could trust me before she showed me anything. No, I think that information is parked where she could have reached it easily. Not in this house. And not at Cranford. I've been over them both inch by inch."

"Oh!" Her eyes grew round with alarm. "What if only Huldah knows—knew—"

He nodded. "That's it. Unless Jud and the D.A. can dig up a safety-deposit box in some Seattle bank, I'm afraid the show's over as far as J.W.'s claims are concerned. Or anyone's."

27

Thursday Afternoon, January 24

Nan straightened stiffly, resting on her shovel. Behind her the tiled walk she had cleared of snow lay red and shining with moisture in the sun. Almost as much lay ahead, packed with trampled snow and ice to be cleared.

She knew she should go in now. Her knees were trembling, and the warm glow her first exertions had generated in her body had gone. Cold was creeping deeper and deeper into her. And the shovel growing steadily heavier. But firm within her was determination not to re-enter that still house till Dyke returned.

Even though he was largely responsible for its stillness today!

He himself had closed up like a clam last night the moment he'd said, "The show's over." While she lay wide-eyed and sleepless in their bed, he had spent the night pacing back and forth in their sitting room. To the sound of that pacing she had finally fallen into troubled sleep. When she woke, he was gone. Leaving her alone.

Not really alone. Fleur was in the house—but shut away in her own room with David. Eileen was there—behind her in a living-room window—sketching. Beulah was there—in the kitchen.

Angrily she seized her shovel, thrust it against the hard-packed snow. Ice had formed beneath it, and she had to shove again and again to break even a few inches free.

She wished she could shove it into the entire Wales clan. Including Dyke.

Dyke, with that brass wedge, had given the sheriff the first concrete weapon against Ruby. But it was Fleur—ripping open her scarf—who had supplied him with the most convincing and powerful ammunition. And the others, every one of them, in that long discussion following Fleur's disclosure, had helped to build a black and solid case against Mrs. Devens.

But this morning, no!

Their sole concern now was for the Wales name. Apparently no one last night had entertained the thought that this was more than a private affair, to be aired and then wrapped away forever within the walls of the Madrona Place stronghold.

The Wales name in the papers! On the radio! The Wales name linked with murder! That to them was the real crime.

All morning reporters had been at the doors. But no Wales had responded to their rings and knocks. She had had to answer; answer the rings and knocks, at least. But not their questions.

That seemed to have pleased them just as well. They had stared at her with prying, knowing eyes. One of them had whistled. One had called her Sister. Unable to penetrate inside the latched screen door, they had wandered about the grounds, taken photographs of the house from every angle. Finally, like a yelping pack of hounds, they had found the woods path, followed it to the trees and vanished from sight.

Dyke had been blamed for that invasion, too!

"These Wales!" she muttered aloud and emphasized her feelings with sharper thrusts at the ice.

She straightened shortly to ease the ache in her back, pull off a glove to blow on numbed fingers.

With her hand halfway to her lips, she stiffened. Turned her head slowly.

That sound—that soft, dreadful sound she and Dyke had heard—aeons ago, it seemed now—had touched her ears, faded. While she stood motionless, it came again, died away.

And today, as on that late Monday afternoon, there was no wind! And today, as then, she stood almost on the very spot where that sound had stopped them before!

Just ahead in a straight line stood the madrona tree, its bark faintly pink against the white snow. To right and left stretches of settling snow spread over the lawns, packed in crazy patterns by the prowling feet of reporters and photographers.

She thrust her shovel into the snow she had banked beside the walk, pivoted slowly. The sound came again. Diffused, so diffused, she could not guess its direction.

The house was before her now, slightly to her left. On the right, more lawns, broken by massive, leafless maples, bounded by gardens, with withered stalks of perennials showing above the snow. Beyond them, the west orchard rolling upward to the crest of the hill.

Her eyes sought the cluster of tall firs. The disheveled branches hung motionless now, almost free of the snow that had weighted them.

The better to see, she pushed slowly across the lawn. Stopped when she reached the gardens. The widow maker could not have made that sound, she saw then. The widow maker was gone. Must have fallen during the storm.

Nevertheless she pushed clumsily through the snow toward the firs, sinking again and again into snow that sifted coldly over the tops of Fleur's galoshes. Birds still clamorous in the apple trees rose into short flights at her approach, returned to settle on the branches when she passed on.

Stubbornly on. Her curiosity about the sound was waning, but not her determination to remain outdoors.

There was really nothing to see when she reached the firs. Just a long-dead black branch at their feet, half buried in snow.

She kicked at it idly as she looked across the grounds to the garage and barn and chicken house. The ghostly groan could hardly have come from them. They were too prosaic. Also, too far away.

Starting back, she followed a twisting course as she sought smoother footing on the uneven ground. Back on the lawn, she stopped.

The well head halfway between her and the boardwalk was an odd sight, its pyramid lopsided now as the snow packed and settled. Could the sound have come from there? Wells had strange echoes. Curiosity revived, she changed her course again to reach it.

For a moment she stood beside it, hesitating to mar its whiteness. The snow was just right for molding—would make a marvelous snowman for David. Tomorrow she'd make one.

Stooping, she swept her hand across the base of the pyramid, uncovering the ends of two or three planks. Then, hands cupped about her eyes, she bent lower to peer into the dark depths.

Nothing but a pale silver shimmer of thin ice, dusted here and there with snow, met her eyes. Ice so thin that the ebony of the water beneath it showed through. Nothing at all to be heard.

She stood up, looking about again. Tree shadows were long on the lawns. The clamor of the birds had thinned. Beyond the orchard the sun was not sinking but vanishing behind thickening gray skies. And she was cold and tired and bored.

Her determination to remain outside until Dyke returned weakened. After all, she had two warm rooms of her own now. She didn't need to expose herself to either Eileen's or Beulah's barbed resentment, or intrude on Fleur.

At the entrance porch she stamped the snow from Fleur's galoshes, kicked them off and left them there. Beulah would disapprove, she knew. Disapprove also of the shovel left standing upright in the snow. Let her! She disapproved of Beulah, Eileen—all the Wales except Fleur.

As she pulled herself up the stairs by the rail, she wasn't sure she even approved of Fleur.

Dawdling through a hot bath and dressing, her disapproval of Fleur expanded. It wasn't natural for a young woman, only twenty-eight, to spend so much time alone. Well, not alone. But even with David, sweet as he was. It wasn't good for David, either, to have so much attention.

She could understand, of course, why Fleur found no pleasure in either Eileen's or Beulah's company. But after all, Fleur had practically begged Dyke and her to remain. Now Fleur appeared to place her—Nan!—in the same category with the rest. She knew that wasn't fair. Fleur was worried and unhappy. She had made the effort—and successfully—to lock her grief for Huldah in her own breast. Perhaps she couldn't do that—yet—with this new catastrophe Ruby had brought on the house. Just the same, though she couldn't say what she'd feel or do under similar circumstances, Nan was sure she wouldn't hide herself away as Fleur was doing.

She was sick to death of all this inaction. Of this isolation. It was all right for Dyke. He had something to do. He could go into Seattle, move around, see people. Feel alive. She couldn't, and didn't.

As she moved restlessly about the room, New York with all its noise and rush rose before her like an enchanted city. And the guest suite shrank to the dimensions of a prison cell. What could she do here? Read? Write letters? Work on that pull-over for Dyke? The very idea bored her to distraction.

Why didn't Dyke come? It was almost five. He usually was back from Seattle before Peggy and Thor got home. And she'd heard Peggy enter her room some time ago.

Perhaps he had come. She opened the bedroom door, stood listening; feeling, rather. Somehow she could always tell when Dyke was in the house. He wasn't now.

Light from the room behind her illumined the corridor as far as the stair well. Beyond that was darkness, deepening to the blackness of another well.

In sudden decision she switched off her light. She'd had enough of stillness. She'd go down to the dining room, listen to the radio. Get New York, if she could.

Carefully feeling her way past the stair well, she followed the corridor wall. At last her hand found the latch to the narrow back-stairs door. As it swung inward, from somewhere a breath of icy air crept about her ankles. And incredibly, as her hand sought the light switch, a whiff of incense fluttered on the air.

Her hand brushed the switch, went on to grasp wildly at the smooth wall. Then she was falling, headlong, down those narrow, steep black stairs. For a moment she knew flashing pain, then merciful darkness.

28

Friday Morning, January 25

"Nan! Nan! Nan, darling! You're all right now. You can hear me. Open your eyes, dear. Try to speak."

Over and over the words came, faintly, in a gentle rhythm. Nan saw rather than heard them. They danced like little white notes of light in the darkness where she still swayed. Dyke's words. In Dyke's voice, hoarse with weariness and worry.

Over and over those words, or variations of them, played those little white tunes against the blackness. But deep down in a timeless pit she swayed, indifferent.

Gradually, however, in spite of her inertia, those words in that voice were lifting her. Moving her slowly at first, then faster, upward between intangible ebony walls. Her speed increased. She was rushing now. Rushing into light.

Fear gripped her. She might shoot out into space; be lost in that light. And she had no weight, no power to stop that rushing. No hands, either, to grasp those nebulous walls. She knew that. She'd known it a long time. Known it since her hand felt for the light switch. Walls without substance, yet smooth and cool.

But when she reached for that switch, fell, she hadn't been able to make a sound. Now she knew she could. Muscles in her throat worked convulsively. She parted her lips to scream.

A gasp of relief, half a sob, beside her and Dyke's hand pressed lightly on her mouth.

Her eyes flew open. Bright with indignation. Then filled with tears as she saw Dyke's face above hers, pale, anxious.

"Welcome, back, Mrs. Holliman." He couldn't say more. Sitting down beside her, one hand on hers on the bed, he wiped a handkerchief over his face with the other. "Lord, Nan, you gave me a scare."

"Why?"

Relief choked him. "You're practically well, darling. You may have a battered head, a sprained arm, and assorted bruises, but if you can ask why, you'll do."

She tried to move her right arm, lay still, quivering with pain. "I'm hurt."

"Yes, darling. But not badly, really. Don't move, then it won't hurt, much."

"What happened?"

"Don't you remember? You fell, hon. Fell and slid down the back stairs. Yesterday. Yesterday afternoon."

She looked at him blankly. Tried to shake her head. That hurt too. Her left arm seemed all right. She lifted that hand to her head, found it capped with bandages.

"Don't talk. Don't move," he said hurriedly. "Drink this." He brought a glass of something to her, bent straws so she could sip it.

"There," he said when she had taken half of it. "Sleep now."

"No. Tell me."

"But darling, I don't know. No one knows. Thor found you all in a heap on your head when he came up from the basement after a shower about six yesterday. I got back just as he was carrying you in here. Lord, I was scared— you were so white. You aren't now, hon. You're like something Eileen might paint in blacks and blues and greens, and purples. Thor went for a doctor. It seemed hours before he came back with one. And we didn't dare to touch you till he came. But no bones are broken. Thank those narrow stairs for that. After a bad crack on the head when you struck, you must have slid the rest of the way."

"The light switch—"

With difficulty he repressed his eagerness, repeated, "The light switch?"

Her eyes went blank again. "I don't know. I don't remember."

"Don't try, then. It doesn't matter. I'm here. You're all right. I won't leave you again."

On that assurance, she lay quiet, his hand under hers, then drifted off to sleep.

When she woke, the sunlight was gone. Dyke, too. But in the soft light of a table lamp in the sitting room she could see him, head bent, listening. Listening to the sheriff's deep rumble.

"Maybe you're right, Holliman. Maybe now I'm ready at last to believe murder could get into my county, I'm willing to believe anything. But there can't be any harm in asking a few questions. If nothing comes of them, then that's that."

"You haven't said what you expect to accomplish by asking them."

"Well, the doc said she was suffering more from shock than from that fall. She was unconscious from some time before six last night till almost ten this morning. Say, sixteen hours. That's a long time—for a fall downstairs."

"That's why I'd rather not bother her."

"'Spose not. But what if your wife didn't lose her balance? What if someone tripped or pushed her? What if she saw who did it? Wouldn't you want to know it?"

They were talking about her! The sheriff and Dyke. Intrigued, Nan risked that pain in her head to move it so that both ears could function.

"I know," the sheriff drawled on. "No one was around, at least not to hear her when she fell. Miss Fleur—giving David a bath, could hear nothing because of the running water. Peggy Wales—also under a shower. Mrs. Bundy—in the kitchen, an electric beater going full tilt. Eileen Wales—in the living room, making what she calls a sketch; too far away."

Nan could imagine Jud ticking the names off on his big brown fingers.

"Thor wasn't even home. He says anyway that Mrs. Holliman must of already fallen before he came in through the basement door. Otherwise her fall would have sounded down there like a ton of bricks dropping."

"Yes? That accounts for everyone, doesn't it?"

"Yes. But I've got another idea. Mrs. Devens!"

"Mrs. Devens! But she's been gone a week. More than a week."

"That's why I'm thinking about her now. Listen. She tries to take her own life that Tuesday night. Maybe she intended to go through with it. Maybe she didn't. Anyway she takes advantage of the excuse it gives her to refuse to go into Seattle to Huldah's funeral service. By the time you and your wife get back from Cranford, she's skipped."

"Yes."

"Well, you can't go far around here without taking a bus or a taxi. No bus driver remembers seeing her since a week ago Tuesday night. They were used to her Tuesday and Thursday trips, would have remembered if she'd ridden with them on Wednesday. She didn't call the Laketon taxi or pick it up in the village. And it ain't likely a woman like her'd thumb a ride on the highway. No truck'd

stop for her anyway. And private cars are either filled with
war workers going or coming from the shipyards. Or their
wives going or coming around Wales Center."

"What's your idea, then?"

"This. Mrs. Devens may still be around here somewhere. May even have been in this house yesterday. It's
no trick, as Thor said, to get in and out unseen by that
basement door. She may not only have been in this house
yesterday but in that dark hall out there. Maybe your wife
caught sight of her somewhere. Maybe touched her in the
dark. That'd account for shock, wouldn't it? That would
account too for why Thor found her on her head at the
foot of those stairs. Mrs. Devens could take no chances—"

"But she couldn't be wandering around the country—
not in this weather."

"Wouldn't need to. Just west of this hill is a whole col-
ony of war workers' homes. A lot of 'em take in roomers.
If she got into one of 'em Wednesday, she'd be as good as
sealed in a vault for the week that storm lasted. Yesterday
was the first time people could get out. And yesterday, remember," the sheriff underlined the words, "was the first
time hews about Huldah's death and Mrs. Devens' disappearance hit the papers and the radio. The radio got it out
first—about noon."

Dyke nodded. "You mean she'd have to get out—fast?"

"Yeah. And maybe she wanted more than she'd taken
when she skipped. Came back here—"

"I doubt that."

"Ever look in Miss Fleur's garage or barn? Or the apple
house?"

"If you're thinking of the furniture Mrs. Devens stored
in them, yes."

"Must be enough stuff in that garage and barn to fur-
nish eight or ten rooms. Sure looks as if she'd come to

stay, don't it?" The sheriff's rumble changed. "What I'm getting at—someone was in that garage—barn, too—yesterday. Going through that stuff."

"Oh, come! I can't see a woman like Mrs. Devens—"

"Maybe she wanted something—or maybe she wanted to destroy something. In the apple house there's a stove. Thor says no one's been in there for weeks—perhaps since last fall. But I was in it today. And someone's been there— had a fire in that stove—since yesterday. And not anyone from this house, either. Unless it was you." Nan heard a smile come into his voice. "And I don't think it was."

"You're right. But why that elfin touch—and smile?"

"Because what was burned was more of that stuff you smell on almost everything Mrs. Devens owned. And in her room. Even here it seems to me I get a whiff of it occasionally."

"Incense!" Dyke's head went back. Then he leaned forward, shaking it. "There must be some explanation for that fire, but I can't accept that one. Look here, Sheriff, have you ever thought the woman may still be here—may never have left the grounds—alive?"

"Dead?" Jud's silence fairly boiled for a moment. "Yeah. I've thought of that. That's why I combed this place pretty thoroughly. Not a sign."

"That you've seen. Or I've seen. But if Nan, wandering around yesterday—found her—that would explain shock, why she can't seem to remember—"

"If she could tell us where she went! Those blasted newspapermen and photographers were all over the place yesterday. Hard to tell which are her tracks or theirs. *Or Mrs. Devens'.*"

"You still insist she's alive?"

"Too easy to think anything else. Until you got a body or something to say where the body is. Sure, I think she's alive. You got any real grounds for thinking different?"

"No. I just think, period. She wasn't a smart woman, nor a very courageous one. And she didn't have much more than that twenty-five dollars, I imagine. And couldn't get more."

"I know. She didn't sell that house of hers. She lost it to taxes and other claims. We've gone into all that. But these mousy women, they can be tough. Look at the way she hung on here."

Dyke shrugged, rose impatiently. "All right. What are your questions? I'll ask them if Nan seems brighter when she wakes up."

29
Friday Afternoon, January 25

When the sheriff had tiptoed heavily away, Dyke came in to stand beside the bed, looking down at his wife. Nan's eyes were closed, and for a moment she kept them that way, smiling to herself at thought of his surprise when she answered each question aptly.

He didn't ask them. Instead when she opened her eyes as he turned on a lamp, he said, "Hungry?"

She was, she realized. Ravenous. Minutes passed while he ran down to the kitchen, returned with a tray, fed her spoonful by spoonful. Minutes more while he fussed about, plumping pillows, making her comfortable.

Impatiently she bit into her swollen lower lip. Finally prodded, "Aren't you going to ask them?"

He turned on another lamp to see her clearly. "You— brat! You were awake! Listened!"

"Of course. It was fascinating. Jud should write for the movies." She sighed. "I couldn't wait to hear his questions. They'd be cosmic, I thought. And I'd be the key something or other to solve the great mystery."

"You aren't? Well, that relieves my mind, at least. You didn't see or hear anything?"

"Just some birds."

"Begin at the beginning. I mean, from the minute you left the house yesterday. I know what you did up to that time. And stop the moment you feel tired."

"I didn't do anything but get a shovel from the barn and clean the sidewalk—or half of it. Then I heard that ghastly sound—the one we heard, remember? And tried to locate it."

"Any luck? Where did you go?"

"Not very far. Over to the firs. That widow maker Fleur told me about couldn't have made it. It had fallen. Coming back I thought of the well, looked down there."

He glanced at her quickly, looked away. After a moment, asked casually, "See anything?"

"Just ice. A little snow."

"Ice broken?"

"No. A little snow wouldn't break it."

"You mean ice covered the water everywhere."

"Of course. Solid. That's how I knew the sound hadn't come from the well."

"Probably has some very simple explanation. Thor may know. Then what did you do?"

"Came back to the house. Took a bath. By that time I was so fed up with all this hush-hush, I wanted noise and lots of it. I thought I'd get a band or something good and loud on the radio."

"You didn't see or hear anyone in the corridor?"

"Of course not. That sheriff's an incurable romantic, Dyke. He's never had a murder case before and wants to make Ruby a master mind like something from a thriller. She'll never come back here."

"No. You're right about that." He turned to look out the window, leaned forward to cup his hands, the better to see.

"What's the matter?"

"Nothing. Just Thor—with an armful of wood chunks."

"Let me see."

He laughed, carefully lifted her head to tuck an extra pillow under it, then turned out the lights. "Poor child. You are in a bad way—for excitement!"

They both watched curiously, however, as Thor, a massive silhouette against the snow, paced about below them, dropping his wood blocks several feet apart on a diagonal between the madrona and the house. When he had them all placed to suit him, he turned away, disappeared.

Shortly his footsteps sounded on the stairs. Dyke had just time to turn on the lights when he appeared in the doorway.

He smiled at Nan. "Hello. Nice to have you with us again." Of Dyke he asked, "Where's Jud? I thought he was with you."

"Somewhere outside, I guess. Anything I can do?"

"You've done your part. Helping me sharpen that ax."

"You're not cutting down that madrona tonight?"

"Won't take long. Still half an hour or so till dark. And Jud's an expert with ax and saw."

"Thor!" Fleur's soft voice spoke behind him. "You can't. You know you can't do that."

He turned. "I should have done it months ago. You must see that now."

"No. I'll never consent."

"Suppose David had fallen down those stairs. Would you have wanted him to wait—as Nan had to do—for hours while I drove round the country, locating a doctor? We've got to have a phone, Fleur. If the only way we can have one is on the company's terms, then we're going to get it that way."

"I forbid it." She pressed by him to enter the room and appeal to Dyke. "He can't do it against my wishes, can he?"

"I agree with Thor," Dyke said slowly. "But if you're making a legal point there, no, I suppose he can't. You're the head of the house."

Thor smiled oddly. "I won't argue that—unless it's necessary. It's up to you, Fleur."

She remained silent, her eyes intent on his. Then she moved back, to place a hand on his arm.

"Thor, dear, I'm sure there's some other way. Dyke's a lawyer. He could see the phone people for us, explain how much that tree means. You're upset, because of Nan. That was dreadful. But it wasn't lack of a phone that was responsible. It was lack of lights in the corridor. After this we'll always have some rooms lighted up here, their doors open—"

"After this we'll have a phone."

Fleur's hand dropped. "I forbid it."

The healthy color drained slowly from Thor's quiet face. "You prefer the madrona—to David?"

She stepped back to look at him incredulously. "You wouldn't!"

"I would. I won't go on this way, Fleur. It isn't right for David. Or for me."

"But it won't be long now, Thor. This must all work out soon. You'll see."

"You've been saying that for three years, Fleur. And I was fool enough to believe it. I'm sorry the madrona has to be the issue. But something had to be sometime. This is it."

Dyke and Nan watched in increasing embarrassment. But neither Thor nor Fleur was aware of them now.

Suddenly Thor turned. "Peggy!" he called.

Her door down the corridor opened with amazing promptness. She came down the corridor swiftly to stop just outside the door. "Find Beulah and Eileen, will you? Bring them here. David, too."

He said nothing more. Nor did Fleur. She had backed away from him to a window, faced him, still unbelieving.

Eileen came lightly down the corridor from her room. Beulah up the front stairs. Last came Peggy, David in her arms.

At sight of Thor he shouted gleefully, stretched out his hands. "Tor! Tor! Ride. Ride me."

Thor took the child from Peggy, smiled down at him. "Not now, David. Listen."

David took him literally. Scrambling up his arm like a monkey, he placed a pink ear against Thor's.

Nan gasped, looked at Dyke. But he was expressionless, his veiled eyes fixed on Thor.

She looked again at that strange tableau in the doorway: Thor and David, both so fair, with the same clear light blue eyes, against the silent background of the three tall, dark-eyed Wales women.

Thor took a step forward to turn a little so that he could see everyone.

He said slowly, carefully, "This is a strange time and a strange way to say what I must say now. But I asked you all to come to tell you something you should have known long ago. Fleur is my wife. David is my son."

Beulah's eyes, bright with shock, moved instantly to Fleur.

Peggy stood rigid and white as an image.

Eileen laughed softly. "At last. May we congratulate you now?"

"No." Thor's voice was level. "That's all. I just—just wanted you to know. I am the head of this house."

He did not move or speak again until they had gone.

Fleur remained by the window, straight and silent, too. She no longer wore a scarf about her throat. Now it formed a slender firm support for her proudly held head.

After a moment Thor turned and left the room, David contentedly quiet against his shoulder.

"Sit down, Fleur," Dyke suggested. "And don't look like that. Nothing very terrible has happened. Thor's a mighty fine fellow. And you have a mighty fine son."

Nan remained speechless. Thor was a mighty fine fellow.

But Fleur—Fleur had not been trained to marry a young Norwegian farm boy. Remembering Grandfather Wales' and Huldah's ambition for Fleur, she couldn't think at the moment of any man who really could meet their specifications.

Fleur still stood in the window. "He had no right to speak now," she said as if to herself. "He promised me. And he has no right to cut down that madrona when he knows how much it means to me."

"Perhaps it means a great deal to more than you, Fleur." Dyke drew an envelope from a pocket, shook out on his hand a natural-wood button.

As he held it out, she moved close to look. "Where did you get that? It's Huldah's lucky piece!"

"Where did she get it?"

"Grandfather Wales made it for her. He cut six of those buttons out of a branch for her before I was born. She used to change them from one sweater to another as she knitted them. Some broke. One or two were lost. That's the last one. She always carried it with her."

She came out of the half daze in which she spoke with a jerk. Stricken with some thought, stepped back. "She must have had it—"

Dyke nodded. "I picked it up in the broom patch the day after Huldah was found there. Sent it in to Seattle. I was curious about this button. I still am. For I know something about it now. It's made of madrona wood."

She sank into the chair he had placed for her as if her knees would no longer support her. For minutes she sat silent, absorbed with some inner emotion. Suddenly she sprang to her feet.

"Dyke! Dyke! Tell Thor it's all right. Tell him to hurry. It's all right."

When he stood unmoving, she cried, "Don't you see, Dyke? The madrona! That's where the records must be. That button's a message—from Huldah—to me!"

30

Friday Night, January 25

With Fleur and Dyke, Nan watched from the window Thor's strong arms swinging the ax in rhythmic strokes. Each fell precisely into the triangle the first stroke had cut.

That first stroke must have reached Jud's ears, for, almost instantly, he appeared on the run. Now he stood, feet wide apart, hands on hips, watching critically.

When Thor propped the ax, Jud was beside him with a long, deep-toothed, double-handled saw. Soon its whine rose to the trio in the window. By the time the old madrona was swaying, Beulah and Eileen had joined them. Downstairs, David's excited yells grew louder and shriller. With Peggy he watched from a living-room window.

Darkness was closing in as the upper branches began to tremble, the whole tree to sway. Then, as if of its own accord, the madrona, feeling itself freed, leaped—fell. The crash sent snow in a long line flying high in air. When it settled, the tree rested accurately on the wood blocks Thor had laid down to receive it.

"Smart feller, Thor," Dyke applauded. His voice had something of the wistful small boy's, kept from a circus.

Fleur, turning to hurry downstairs and out to the tree, looked back. "You go, Dyke. I'll stay with Nan. Take a

flashlight. Look carefully. You'll find something. I don't
know where or how."

She sat down quietly beside Nan. "Darling, how
thoughtless we've all been! You are supposed to have rest
and quiet."

"A little rest and quiet wouldn't do you any harm," Nan
retorted. "But I think the excitement's been good for me.
Even my head forgot to ache. And I'm thrilled about you
and Thor, Fleur. Really, I am. I like him."

"You're wondering, aren't you, why we never told? It
was my fault, of course. Now I can see I was wrong. But—
Oh, I was just a silly fool. That's all. Deluded like all the
rest of the Wales—by the name. Grandfather Wales, Granny, and Huldah most of all had impressed on me, from
the time I was old enough to understand, that I was something pretty special. At college, you remember, I never
let myself go—over anyone. I didn't dare. I was a terrific
snob. You know that. Outwardly, at least. But inside I was
afraid—afraid no one measured up to Grandfather's standards. Then—"

"Then?" Nan prompted.

Fleur hesitated a moment, went on rapidly as if relieved to be free at last to talk.

"Then I came home for vacation after my junior year.
Thor was here, of course. But I hardly knew him. You remember how young and skinny and shy he was the year before, when you were here? Well, he'd changed in every way.
And he'd worked like a demon on his English. Both because he wanted to and because Huldah stood over him—
you know how she'd be. Grandfather liked him, helped
him, too."

Fleur was silent, remembering. "That summer I had
lots of time to myself. Granny was gone. Grandfather
Wales in bed most of the time. Huldah busy with him and
the house and her eternal canning. Thor looked after the

place, but there wasn't much to do. We spent hours every day swimming, motoring around the country, hiking. Just lying out on the hill somewhere in the sun. Well—that's all. Two young things—in the mood for love, I guess. Summer, moonlight, all for us. In August, Thor had to drive to Spokane on some business for Grandfather. I was to drive with him as far as Wenatchee to visit friends. I didn't. I went on to Spokane, and we were married there. Had a week together. When we got back, I was afraid to tell Grandfather. But we didn't need to tell Huldah. She knew. In fact—I think she'd managed Thor and me like two puppets. She pretended to be furious, but she wasn't."

"You said Thor is the grandson of an old friend of hers in Norway?"

Fleur flushed. "He—he's Huldah's own grandson."

"Huldah's! I always thought she— She called herself Miss Huldah Swenson."

"Perhaps she'd never married. I don't know. At any rate, she'd had a child—a daughter—in Norway. The father was the son of some rich landowner from whom her father rented land. When the baby was born, the father's family made trouble, insisted on Huldah leaving the country. So her mother kept the child and she came to the United States. She worked as nursemaid in New York for some family that brought her to Seattle one summer. But when they were ready to go back, Huldah refused to leave. Grandfather heard of her, brought her out here to Granny—"

Nan listened, silently, sure Fleur was right. Huldah was a shrewd and ambitious woman. To marry her grandson to the granddaughter of the patriarch of Madrona Place would erase the rankling sore in her heart against the landowner in Norway who had scorned her alliance with his son. To Huldah, that would be the ultimate triumph!

Fleur was saying, "Huldah told me to go back to Vassar, that I was quite right not to want to tell Grandfather then, that she'd arrange everything before I came back in the spring. So I didn't tell him. But soon I knew David was coming. I was simply paralyzed with fright. I didn't know what to do. Finally, after Christmas, I wrote Huldah. And she sent me that telegram about Grandfather needing me. I took it to the dean—and left for Madrona Place in good standing."

"But your grandfather was ill."

"Yes. Huldah said he hadn't many months to live. That's why I didn't tell him about Thor."

"But afterwards—when he died—?"

"David was born. I couldn't tell then. You know how small communities gossip. I went to Idaho, to a hospital there. Huldah came, took David straight to Cranford. By that time I didn't want to tell. I knew then I didn't love Thor. I wanted to get a divorce. Huldah wouldn't hear of it. Neither would Thor. He's as proud as she was. And they had a—a gun at my head in David. If I wanted my son, I had to stay with Thor. Last spring I couldn't stand it any longer—"

"That's when you brought her back?"

"She brought him back!" Fleur's soft voice trembled, steadied. "She brought him back to grow up at Madrona Place. To be trained and steeped in it as I had been. She didn't care any more about me or Thor. We had served our purpose. David was everything. David was a Wales *and* a Swenson!"

Shouts came to them from below the window. The sheriff's loudest of all. Then silence, followed by the sharp crack of an ax.

Fleur rose to peer down at three dark figures breaking and pulling branches away from the fallen tree. "They've found something! Oh, thank God!"

She turned, tears streaming down her face, and sped for her room.

The front door burst open. Footsteps pounded up the stairs. Dyke first, the sheriff and Thor behind him.

Nan's eyes widened at sight of the roll in Dyke's hands. It was a long, rolled magazine, she saw when he tried to smooth it out under the lamp on the table beside the bed. An old and faded copy of some woman's household magazine. When Dyke finally persuaded it to open she glimpsed a woman's head on the faded cover, then the words, *The Ladies' Home Journal*.

Opening it, Dyke lifted out a thick sheaf of papers from the center. Smaller sheafs from other pages. Until he had removed each one, no one spoke.

Jud LaRue's eyes actually showed emotion, excitement. He put out a big hand. "I'll take those, Holliman."

He took them from Dyke, his hands shaking so he could hardly hold them. Slowly he read the title on the topmost sheet.

"The last will and testament of James Joseph Wales," he said, softly for him. "Old man Wales' will." He looked up. "But there was a will! Maybe this is a later one! Maybe we'd better get Miss Fleur in here. Or her lawyer, if she has one."

"Dyke's our lawyer," Thor said.

"O.K." The sheriff stopped, repeated, "Our?"

"Our," Thor told him firmly. "Fleur is my wife."

The sheriff's face closed swiftly. "I guess this thing's getting too big for me. Maybe we're moving too fast. I guess I'd better take this up with the D.A."

Dyke took on his tomahawk look, but he spoke amicably enough. "You're doing all right, Jud, I'd say. Except on one point, of course. But if you're going to take those records into Seattle, I'm going along."

"I'm doing all right on that, too," the sheriff told him flatly. "She'll turn up. You'll see. She can't get far." He tucked the papers into the magazine and the magazine firmly under his arm. "Let's go."

Dyke hesitated.

"I'll stay with Nan," Thor assured him.

When they had gone, Thor sat down heavily in the chair, by the window. He was tired, bewildered, unhappy, Nan saw, glad for a time to be quiet. She did not speak, and gradually his face cleared.

"What have I done, Nan?" he asked uneasily, "I chop down a tree to get a telephone and bring a personal situation that's been driving me crazy to an end. Instead, I seem to have set off something else that may be worse. What's going on and what is it that Jud and Dyke don't agree on? Does Dyke think Ruby's managed to get away?"

Nan looked at him uncertainly. If the sheriff or Dyke had said nothing to him, perhaps she shouldn't. Yet Thor had done everything he could from the moment he learned of Ruby's disappearance to find her. Surely he had a right to know what they knew.

"Jud believes Ruby's still alive, Thor. That she may even have been in this house—in the corridor—when I fell downstairs. Dyke thinks she's dead."

Thor's head jerked back. As he looked at her his eyes turned to blue ice. "Maybe Jud's right. Wait."

He jumped up, sped down the hall, was back in a moment, a small black wool scarf in his hand.

"This was on the floor just inside my door when I got back there after the excitement over getting a doctor for you had died down. I picked it up, tossed it on a shelf, forgot it. But ever since I've been plagued by incense. Smell this!"

Memory of an icy breath touching her ankles as she reached for that light switch flashed across Nan's mind. And then another—that whiff of incense! Thor's room was icy cold. If Ruby had opened it to slip in—or out!

"If she was there, I didn't see her. It was too dark. But perhaps she thought I did."

"And pushed you. As Jud thinks she did to Huldah." He nodded. "She couldn't take a chance on your seeing her."

They were still discussing the idea when Dyke returned unexpectedly. He sniffed at the black scarf, listened to their theories.

"It's up to the D.A. now," he said finally. "He'll be here at ten o'clock tomorrow. Tell the others, will you, Thor?"

He waited till Thor was some distance down the stairs before he allowed elation to show, "Boy, what a D.A.!" he said. "Get all the sleep you can tonight, Nan, Mr. Alexander P. Ramsey's going to town on this case—or else!"

31

Saturday Morning, January 26

Dyke's forecast came true an hour before scheduled. On the point of nine Saturday morning, four cars lined up at the stump of the madrona tree. From the smart closed car leading the procession, a small, thin man literally sprang out, stopped to sweep house and grounds with a single glance, then wave a peremptory arm at the second car.

Jud LaRue emerged from it slowly. As slowly walked toward the house. Behind him the small dynamo was waving more men from the two trucks. Big men who gathered about him to listen as he talked and gestured.

Before the sheriff could knock or ring, Thor opened the door. Started to swing out the screened door for him to enter.

Jud shook his head, awkwardly produced a paper. "The D.A.'s here," he rumbled. "Wants to go over Madrona Place, Thor. Be better if you just gave your consent. If not. I have a warrant—"

"Keep it," Thor told him. "Tell him to go—where he likes."

Jud grinned. "I get you. If it's any comfort to you, that's sure where he will go, eventually. Thanks."

He let the screen close, shoved the paper in his pocket. Stepping down from the entrance porch, he waved a hand to the waiting men, then walked slowly to meet them.

For the next half-hour, it seemed to any member of the house, looking out from any window, that a dozen district attorneys were darting about the grounds, each trailed by two or three men. They were in the barn, the garage, even the chicken house. Two crossed the back road, disappeared in the apple house. Other groups tramped methodically over the lawns, shovels or spiked poles in their hands, moved through the orchards.

At nine-thirty the D.A. stood on the entrance porch, placed a firm finger on the bell. Again Thor answered.

"I'm Alexander P. Ramsey. District attorney," he announced. Opening the screen door himself, he stepped into the foyer. "I'd like to talk with Mr. Holliman."

"Mr. Holliman is upstairs," Thor told him calmly. "His sitting room's just at the left—"

"Thank you."

The D.A. rounded him briskly, started upward, turned. His tawny hazel eyes flashed like sparks in his hatchet-shaped face, from Thor's fair hair to his wide-toed shoes. "I'll be ready for you all at ten o'clock."

He was. But not in the living room, where Thor had built up the fire, placed chairs. The Hollimans' sitting room suited him perfectly, when he had had the table moved across the open door to the bedroom where Nan lay, amusedly comparing him with a fox terrier. Even his words came in short, sharp barks.

Mrs. Holliman, he declared, had taken an active part in the case at three points at least—finding the button, appropriating the letter in Huldah Swenson's mailbox, falling downstairs. Her presence was essential. Ergo, the sitting room.

The arrival of Beulah, Eileen, and Peggy at the sitting-room door promptly on the stroke of ten did not discompose him, though they were almost a head taller. Briskly he seated them, made sure he understood which name belonged to whom. Thor arrived shortly with Jud.

Behind them came Fleur, her hands full of stuffed pets. And David with his Oodoo. She stopped in the bedroom door, looked at Nan.

"Can he stay with you? He says he'll play mice and not make a sound."

When Nan nodded, she dropped the animals on the bed, lifted David.

"Why don't you stay here, too, Fleur? You can see and hear all just as well—"

"And be shot at sunset, if not before?" Fleur smiled wanly. "No. I'm going to sit right under his nose so he can see I have nothing up my sleeves."

She kissed David on the top of the head. That was all that was visible. His idea of playing mice was to try to crawl under his Oodoo with all his pets. Since the sweater had its limitations, the problem, Nan could see, was going to keep him absorbed for hours. Fleur looked at the heaving sweater for a moment, turned away.

Another moment and Mr. Ramsey's voice crackled. "Sit here, Mrs. Satterlund. We are now ready to begin, I believe. First, I must confess I have been very remiss to permit this case to drag on as it has. Almost two weeks have elapsed since Huldah Swenson walked out of this house—to her death. In that time we have learned only where she died, how she died, and approximately when. Why she died and at whose hand, we have yet to discover. We shall do that this morning. I am confident that in the records I found here last night in a madrona tree we shall find the answers."

An abrupt protest from Beulah stopped him.

"You mention Mrs. Devens? We shall consider her disappearance and possible bearing on Huldah Swenson's

death in due course, Mrs. Bundy. Now, if you will permit
me—"

He stood behind the small table, his narrow shoulders
arched almost to his ears, very like a teacher faced by a
not-too-bright class. Taking up a handful of papers, he
rapped them smartly on the edge of the table to make
them stand erect.

"This is a copy of the last will and testament of the
late James Joseph Wales, of Madrona Place. Its main text
is similar to that of the original will filed shortly after his
death three years ago. You all know, I believe, that by the
terms of that will all his properties, of whatever nature,
became the properties of his granddaughter, Fleur Wales,
the present Mrs. Thor Satterlund. In conclusion, the will
names Huldah Swenson as executor."

Beulah murmured again. He raised a finger.

"If you please, Mrs. Bundy. Later we will consider what
you have to say. Permit me to finish, first." He glanced at
his wrist watch pointedly. Evidently this meeting had a
schedule, too.

Beulah subsided.

"Two documents, however, were found attached to this
copy of the will. One is a brief statement, signed by the
late Huldah Swenson. It is her written promise to carry
out the terms of the will in accordance with a comprehen-
sive and detailed plan attached."

Mr. Ramsey disposed of will and statement by dropping
them on the table. This time no one ventured to speak.
He looked round the still, unrevealing faces in the sitting
room, then into the bedroom, at Nan, bright-eyed against
pillows. Assured of everyone's attention, he took up another set of papers.

"I hold here Mr. Wales' farsighted program for Madrona Place. Quite rightly, I believe, he saw this area as the

coming scene of great development. He realized the strategic importance of the site at the foot of this hill known as the Crossroads, where Wales Center, the first unit in his plan for a business section there, is now located.

"This plan calls for a survey and plotting of Madrona Place after the war to divide the property into residence streets and boulevards for country places along the lake front and on the crest of this hill. It also provides that this house and three acres remain in the hands of his granddaughter as her residence for as long as she wishes to remain here; to be sold and incorporated in the general estate if she ever desires to leave it. It has other provisions which I will mention later."

Those papers dropped accurately to the table on top of the will. And a third set smacked against the table edge.

"Now!" said the D.A. significantly. "I mention the will and the plan merely as they rebate to these papers—these records—I now hold in my hand. They consist of carefully kept accounts of moneys received, over a period of some twenty years by James Joseph Wales from five different members of his family. Moneys to be invested in the enlargement and upkeep of Madrona Place. With Mr. Holliman's assistance, I have identified representatives of the immediate families of these five relatives who are now—or have been until recently—in this house."

He had no need to ask for silence now. Both rooms were so still, they might have been vacuum-packed. In that stillness his sharp, dry voice cut like whipcracks.

"Each amount is recorded here under, specific dates in five separate accounts. I merely give the totals—and in round numbers. My office is solely concerned with Mr. Wales' business affairs in so far as they relate to the death of Huldah Swenson. That is understood? Very well then. Here are the figures:

"James Wardman Wales, represented by his stepson, Dyke Holliman, $15,000. Mrs. Reginald Bundy, represented by Mrs. Bundy herself, $10,000. John Fulton Wales, represented by his daughter, Eileen Wales, $8,000. Joseph Franklin Wales, represented by his daughter, Margaret, $6,000. And Paul Devens, until a few days ago represented by his wife, known as Ruby Devens, $7,500. Total, $46,500."

"Forty-six thousand dollars!" Beulah could maintain silence, no longer. "For that amount twenty years ago my brother could have bought this entire county—"

Alexander P. Ramsey's iced gaze silenced her. "James Joseph Wales at the time of the first World War owned this house and some thirty acres. He made a modest income growing apples and cherries. The war years for two reasons caused him to abandon fruit production. One was the rapidly growing fruit regions east of the Cascades. The second was his realization that he did not need to work the land. The land left alone would work for him handsomely. He came to that shrewd conclusion as the result of watching the impetus the first World War gave Seattle.

"Mr. Wales' reputation as a man of shrewd judgment is still remembered throughout the Puget Sound region. Perhaps his shrewdest decision—unknown until now—was his plan to permit those who would profit most by his judgment in the future to maintain him and his household until that profit could be realized. He sold his three sons, James, Joseph, and John, his sister, Beulah, and his nephew, Paul Devens, the idea of the coming value of this land.

"On the moneys they supplied him, he bought and sold land until he had acquired this square mile extending from the lake front to the highway half a mile north of this house. In those years the land had almost no value. He was able to carry out his plan, make a profit occasionally. During the last few years, he lived very comfortably."

To anticipate any reactions, Mr. Ramsey raised a hand. "Mr. Wales was shrewd, but he was honest and fair. He knew he might not live to see the day when Madrona Place realized its value. But he kept these records, and he made a fair arrangement by which each of the five members who invested with him in Madrona Place would reap a substantial profit.

"As the man who conceived the project and acquired the land, he reserved fifty-one per cent for himself. That fifty-one per cent now belongs to Mrs. Satterlund. The remaining forty-nine per cent he arranged to be divided among his sons, his sister, and his nephew or their heirs in proportion to their investment."

Turning to Dyke, Mr. Ramsey triangled his narrow black brows. "To expedite matters—from the point of view of my office, Mr. Holliman—may I steal a little of your thunder? The total figures only?"

Dyke nodded.

"Thank you." The D.A. turned back to his now mesmerized audience. "In the course of his visit to Seattle, Mr. Holliman has been approached by an investment syndicate of Seattle businessmen. He will give, you the details later. This syndicate is intensely interested in acquiring Madrona Place. Quite independently of any contact with the late Mr. Wales, it has worked out a development program that in a general way follows his original one. Possibly, however, because they are men of greater experience and knowledge, their plan goes far beyond that of Mr. Wales.

"You may or may not wish to accept the offer this syndicate is prepared to make you through Mr. Holliman. I mention it here to give you an idea of the value of Madrona Place as of this date."

A smile flickered over his thin lips at the impatience his prologue had roused.

"This offer involves the sum of $200,000. Divided according to Mr. Wales' plan, this would realize, roughly, a total of $102,000 for Mrs. Satterlund. The remaining $98,000 would be divided proportionately among the rest of you and Mrs. Devens or your heirs. Since the original investment totaled only $46,500, you can see you are on the verge of realizing a minimum profit of *slightly more than one hundred per cent.*"

The dramatic, not to say sinister, emphasis he gave to the final words fell on the tensely listening ears of his audience like thunder ripping through a silent night. He paused, looked at them a moment, before concluding.

"Murder has often been committed for much less than one hundred per cent profit on a dollar."

32

Saturday Morning, January 26

The tawny eyes lighted as they watched anger and resentment stain every face. "That was simply a general observation, apropos of nothing. For the time being," he assured them.

He glanced approvingly at his watch. Apparently he was ahead of schedule.

"It's said," he smiled, "that many men of certain similar abilities enter one of three professions—the ministry, the theater, or the law. I entered the law, but occasionally I do a bit of acting." He smiled at Mrs. Bundy, Eileen, and Peggy, an erect row on his right. "That is what I was doing some minutes ago when I failed to indicate I had seen any of you before this morning. And why I have never mentioned knowing Mrs. Devens. . . .

"In the past few months they have each called at my office. Each has made the same inquiries, given me almost identical information concerning the reason for their interest in Madrona Place. In addition, I have assembled a rather substantial file on Madrona Place from different offices in the County Courthouse—the office of register of deeds, of the tax commissioner, and so on. This file includes various letters, dating back over a period of years, received from members of the Wales family or their legal representatives in this country, in England, France, and South Africa."

He paused as if expecting comments from his listeners. But they were now either so disciplined or so willing for him to reveal his entire hand that no one gratified him.

"Last of all," he continued after a moment, "came Mr. Holliman. About two weeks ago. Tuesday, January 15, to be exact. We will remember that date for some time as the day when the angriest man ever to enter my office arrived. Mr. Holliman had just discovered the third and most important of three reasons why neither my predecessors in office nor myself were able to be of any real assistance. The first—that the value of Madrona Place until the last two or three years was less than the amount of any of the claims against it. The second—that the claimants, owing to their distance from Seattle, lack of financial resources, and strong family scruples, could not bring their claims into court. And the third—that Madrona Place does not stand and for some years has not stood on the records in the name of James Joseph Wales."

"I didn't know it had been placed in my name, Mr. Ramsey," Fleur declared quickly and firmly. "I didn't know that until after my grandfather died."

"You know now why the property was transferred to you?"

"Yes. Huldah told me—after his death. That is, at first she told me the claims my uncles and aunt and Paul Devens were making were not genuine. That to protect Madrona Place my grandfather seven or eight years ago decided to register the land in my name."

"At first?" Mr. Ramsey repeated. "Does that mean she gave you a second explanation?"

"Last spring," Fleur admitted reluctantly. "Last spring she told me it was true their money had been invested in Madrona Place. But she wouldn't let me see the records she had kept for my grandfather. Or even tell me where they were."

"You continued the policy of silence Mr. Wales and Huldah Swenson had established?" the D.A. asked.

She nodded. "After she convinced me it was too soon then to acknowledge their claims. She said she and Grandfather Wales had foreseen just what has happened. That when any of them—or their heirs—was under financial pressure, they'd try to get their money back. If any one of them was permitted to do so, the others would lose their investments. Not only that, but none of them would make any profit—"

"That isn't true!" Beulah interrupted. "Don't tell me my brother had any part in such a scheme. You and that housekeeper—"

"It is true!" Fleur cried. "They did this for your own good—for all of you. And you aren't even grateful! Even when you know you're not only going to get back the original investment but that investment doubled—if we accept this offer Dyke says he has. But if you'll wait—only three or four years more—you'll gain three or four times—"

"Why wait?" Beulah demanded. "People are clamoring for this land now."

"Because most of these people are only temporary. When the war's over, they'll go back where they came from— leaving rows of cheap little shops and houses. Ruining everything. This can be a beautiful suburb, with restricted homes and small estates, and a real business center. Wales Center isn't a year old, yet it's already serving more than five thousand people. Grandfather Wales spent years and years studying and planning—talking with men who know the Northwest. He was thinking, planning for all of you, as well as for himself—and me."

She turned in her chair to look from Beulah to Eileen to Peggy slowly. "I'm glad the records have been found.

That you can see for yourselves no one wanted to cheat you. But I insist Grandfather and Huldah, too, were right. That I was right, to say nothing—"

"I'm sorry to have to interrupt your defense of your grandfather, Mrs. Satterlund," the D.A. said crisply. His eyes were on the door, on the railing along the stair well, rather, where the head of one of his men and a waving arm were signaling.

"We'll all meet in this room again later. But first I must leave for a few minutes. Then I shall return to talk with each of you privately. I believe we'll get further faster that way."

With a quick half bow, he sped away.

Without a glance for the others, Fleur rose immediately and entered the bedroom to collect David and go on to her own room.

Dyke and Jud looked at each other, then followed the district attorney. Beulah and Eileen left together, talking in low voices as they walked down the corridor to Eileen's room. After a moment Thor, Peggy at his heels, came out of the sitting room, ran down the front stairs.

The foyer door below opened and closed sharply. Then the house was still.

For more than an hour Nan remained alone, gazing uneasily out the window at the line of empty cars. Occasionally one of the D.A.'s men visited a truck to collect another shovel or ax or pole.

Then the front door opened and she heard Mr. Ramsey's clear bark. He was giving directions to half a dozen men for a complete search of the house.

After that, the house was no longer still. Feet sounded everywhere, upstairs and down, as men went through each room. Echoes of doors slamming, drawers being pulled out, shoved in, furniture moved, walls tapped, rolled down the corridor, up the stairs.

She listened angrily. But there was nothing she could do. Anyone could do. Even Jud LaRue. Mr. Ramsey had taken command.

Later she heard his sharp, high voice demanding Fleur. Then he walked briskly past Nan's door, entered the sitting room, closed the connecting door without a glance for her. Shortly Fleur appeared, entered the sitting room. Its door to the hall closed also.

Dyke came slowly up the stairs, looked down at Nan a moment, then sank into the chair by the side window, to look unseeingly across the snow to the firs along the highway.

"What are they looking for?" she prodded finally.

"Anything or nothing, I guess. Ramsey agrees with me that Mrs. Devens can't have left the grounds. But they've taken the place apart—outside and in. Ripped up floors in the barn and apple house, sounded every foot of the garage. Sounded every foot of the grounds, too. Even the trees and the ice in the well. They haven't found a scrap of paper or a mark of any kind to show that anything happened to her—here."

He got up to move restlessly about the room. "They're still at it. And she's got to be here somewhere. She must be here. Think, Nan. If you wanted to do away with yourself—or wanted to do away with someone else—where would you go? What would you do? Somewhere near—in the house or not far from it."

She gazed at him as if he had lost his mind. "I've thought sometimes she might have tried again to kill herself. But Dyke—you talk as if—"

"As if someone may have tried to kill her?" He thrust a chair out of his way roughly. "Why not? Someone tried— and succeeded—in killing Huldah."

"But Mrs. Devens struck her! You all said—"

"Maybe. I'm just guessing—in spite of the advice I gave you. But I can't see that terrified little woman coolly faking suicide Tuesday night, then calmly walking out of this house the next morning—with a black bag—and disappearing."

"She lived in Seattle many years."

"The D.A.'s traced down all her friends. That is, people who knew her in Seattle. She doesn't seem to have had any friends, real friends. He has the whole Pacific coast on the lookout for her. And God knows how much territory to the east. She can't have gone north—into Canada. The line's too well guarded these days. The only other direction is west— and there she'd bump into the Pacific Ocean. But someone would surely have seen her before she reached it. Not a soul has spotted her in any direction. She's got to be here!"

He was still moving about when Fleur appeared in the hall outside. She stood for a moment, one hand braced on the stairwell railing, then straightened her shoulders and walked quietly past the door to her own room. Almost immediately Beulah came down the corridor, entered the sitting room, closed the door.

The searching and questioning went on all morning. At noon Mr. Ramsey collected all but one or two of his entourage, led the cars to Laketon for a quick lunch. Before one o'clock they were back, the men to continue their search, the D.A. his questions.

By four o'clock the men were gathering about the trucks. Standing in small groups, talking, looking back at the house and grounds, to shake their heads and talk again.

A little after four Peggy emerged from the sitting room, half crying with anger and exhaustion. She was the last of the household to be questioned.

Shortly the door between bedroom and sitting room opened. Mr. Ramsey appeared in it. Behind him, Jud LaRue loomed.

"God! Holliman," the district attorney said angrily, "if I didn't know Huldah Swenson had been dead forty-eight hours before you reached Seattle, I'd pin this thing on you. These Wales Amazons! They're made of steel. Questions slide off them like water off a teal. Either they're all in this and guilty as hell, or I've been needlessly harrowing the innocent."

Jud LaRue sighed gustily, mopped his face with a wadded handkerchief. Irritated, the D.A. turned.

"What have you got to sigh about? We've proved your point for you, haven't we? Mrs. Devens isn't here!"

He turned back to pick up his papers and notes, stuff them into his brief case. He was halfway into his coat, his hat hanging from his teeth, when the sheriff sighed again.

"Just a minute, D.A." He seemed embarrassed to go on, but under that irascible gaze he found his tongue. "I'm funny, I guess. But the more this hunting and questioning proved me right, the more I think I might be wrong. Before you call it a day, I'd like to ask Mrs. Holliman some questions about that well—"

"The well! You saw yourself the ice is frozen solid. Jake almost broke a spear on it." He looked at the sheriff's stolid, set face, shrugged, tossed his hat to the table. "Well, go ahead then."

Nan tensed as the sheriff walked slowly into the bedroom. He stood a long moment looking at her with those impenetrable blue eyes.

"Yesterday you told your husband that when you looked down that well Thursday afternoon the ice was solid. That right?"

Relieved at the simplicity of his question, Nan told him promptly, "It was. There wasn't a break in it."

"So solid you couldn't see the water anywhere?"

"Of course I could see it. Under the ice. Wherever there wasn't snow on it."

The district attorney moved like a cat to the bed, to fix his eyes on her, unblinking. Jud didn't move, yet somehow he seemed to stand right over her.

"You could see water under the ice? Through solid ice?"

"The ice wasn't thick. Thin—like what we used to call rubber ice when I was small. It was frozen solid to the walls everywhere, of course, but underneath it the water showed black."

The sheriff turned only his head to look at the district attorney. They faced one another blankly for a long moment. Then Mr. Ramsey sped for the sitting room, caught up his hat.

"Call the men," he barked as he raced for the stairs. "Tell Jerry to get into that diving suit."

Jud gave Nan a dumfounded look, lumbered after him.

When they were alone, Dyke said solemnly to his wife, "How's that arm? We'd better be prepared to make a quick getaway?"

"But I told you the ice was frozen solid," she said, bewildered. "It was."

"And I told Jud exactly what you told me—that the ice you saw was frozen solid. The difficulty is, hon, that you meant it was frozen across. To Jud—and I guess he's right—solid means down—how thick the ice was. It's frozen solid both ways now. We've had a freezing forty-eight hours since you saw it. But if it was only frozen solid *across* but not *down* on Thursday, that's— Look!"

Nan looked. An odd procession laden with ladders, ropes, a long basket, was straggling up the tiled walk from the trucks. Behind it came two men, assisting a third. The third was garbed from head to toe in rubber.

33
Saturday Afternoon, January 26

An hour passed before the men shuffling round the open well head stiffened, then moved forward as one man to bend over the rim, peering downward. The district attorney and sheriff, standing a little apart, abandoned their conversation to hurry to look too.

What they saw galvanized them all into activity. Four men began to back slowly, pulling carefully on the ropes that extended from their hands down into the black water. Others bent over the opening to grasp the basket that rose dripping into view.

When it had been lifted out onto the snow, they stood about it for two breaths. One threw a blanket over it, and they all turned hastily away.

Half a dozen of them hurried then to help the man in the rubber suit up the final rungs of the ladder. Clumsily they hoisted him out of the well, stripped the water-glistening suit from him. He stepped free, shook himself, turned away.

Basket and diver were taken away. Two men hurriedly replaced the planks over the well head, sped after them to the trucks. Ramsey and the sheriff lingered, the D.A. talking and gesturing rapidly. Then he went on to his car. Jud LaRue started for the house.

Dyke left the open window of the sitting room out of which he had leaned at a perilous angle to follow proceedings. "I'll be back," he called to Nan as he reached the stairs.

No one else appeared in the foyer. He opened the front door. The sheriff, putty-faced, staggered in.

Silently Dyke waved him to a chair before the fire, hurried away for whisky. LaRue gulped it down, shook his head as if he too were emerging from water.

"God, Holliman! I never bargained on anything like this."

"You found her!"

"Yeah."

"Bag, too?"

Jud shook his head.

"Any ideas—what happened?"

Eyes on the fire, the sheriff was silent. After a moment he said, "Suicide, I guess."

Dyke pursed his lips in a soundless incredulous whistle. "You think she packed that bag to walk from the house to the well? First, hiding it so skillfully a dozen men couldn't find it?"

"I'm past thinking."

"What does Ramsey think, then?"

Jud lumbered to his feet, drawing his hand across his mouth. "The D.A. thinks there are two ways of skinning a cat."

"Meaning—if anything?"

A horn honked peremptorily outside. LaRue picked up his heavy cap and mittens. "Meaning that Mrs. Devens committed suicide. But someone in this house wants it to look like murder."

"Good lord! Why?"

"Yeah. Why?" As the horn sounded again, LaRue turned for the archway. "Maybe someone thinks murder would be a good way of getting rid of Miss Fleur, eh? Maybe you all aren't satisfied with your forty-nine per cent—"

"You can't be serious! You can't think one or all of us would try to pin a murder on Fleur!"

"No? Well, you asked me what the D.A. says—thinks." He pulled his cap down over his thick black hair, drew on the heavy mitts. "If you're a smart guy, Holliman, you'll keep an eye on Miss Fleur. See that nothing happens to her before morning." He stooped, dropping his voice. "Could be, if someone gets the idea we're sure it's suicide, they might try—"

As Thor opened the kitchen door to the foyer, he straightened. "Well, I guess we're through here. For today, at least. Night, Thor."

He pulled open the front door, stepped out, letting the screen door slam behind him.

Nothing happened to Fleur that night. Nothing happened, period, at Madrona Place until early Sunday afternoon. Then the district attorney's smart car, followed by Jud LaRue's hard-driven coupé, drew up once more beside the stump of the madrona.

To the seven haggard adults in the house their arrival was almost welcome. Anything was better than hour after hour of silent suspense, of waiting, wondering, fearing.

The questions began again. One after the other, Fleur, Beulah, Eileen, Peggy, Thor, Dyke entered the Hollimans' sitting room to go over and over again their actions, observations, even their thoughts from Saturday, January 12, on.

When they emerged, exhausted, shaken with resentment for the D.A.'s driving, insistent questions, none was any wiser than when he entered. What was the district attorney trying to prove? That Huldah had been murdered? They thought that had been established. That it was Ruby who struck her with that brass wedge, left her to die in

the broom patch? That too, they thought, had been established.

Now the body of Ruby Devens had been found in the
well. A suicide, obviously, even though the black bag—if
there had been a black bag—had not been found. Yet one
moment Mr. Ramsey's questions implied suicide, the next,
murder, and in still a third, suicide, manipulated to look
like murder.

When they were released, each entered the bedroom to
voice his confusion to Dyke. As obviously, they expected
him to do something, to free them from the D.A.'s per-
secution, to free the house of the fearful, nameless men-
ace that threatened them all. Dyke could only shake his
head. "I can do nothing until one of you is charged with
some crime, or I am myself. I'm in on that forty-nine per
cent, remember. I wasn't here when Huldah died. But I
was when Ruby Devens went down that well."

"But if Ramsey himself thinks it was suicide—" Thor
protested. "Hell, we're going round in circles."

"When the black bag disappeared, then," Dyke qualified, and smiled wryly. "Nan and I could have buried it
or hidden it anywhere between this house and Huldah's in
Cranford that Wednesday morning, remember. Or I could
have disposed of it somewhere when I drove in to Seattle
in the evening. For that matter, so could any of you—
you've all been out of the house since Wednesday morning,
had opportunity to get rid of that bag."

"But Ruby was alive, sleeping in her own bed when
I last saw her," Beulah reminded him. "I couldn't have
known—"

"That's what you say," Dyke pointed out, added hastily: "From the D.A.'s point of view, I mean. No one saw
you see her asleep. That goes for the rest of you. No one
can prove your statements that you didn't go into Ruby's

room at all. No one can say he saw Fleur take that coffee in to her, heard her talking with Ruby—"

"What can we do?" Fleur asked helplessly. "If he won't believe us—"

"Answer his questions. And wait," Dyke advised. He rose when LaRue opened the door into the bedroom, nodded to him.

As he went in and the door closed behind him, Thor came out the sitting room's hall door and, without a glance into the bedroom, went on down the corridor. Fleur rose quickly to follow him. One by one the others slipped away.

Nan was alone when the door to the sitting room opened again. Dyke, followed by Mr. Ramsey and Jud LaRue, walked in to line up at the foot of the bed, looking at her.

"Mrs. Holliman," the district attorney said after a moment, "I haven't asked you any questions, believing that anything you knew, your husband knew—or could learn. But now I need your help."

He walked round to seat himself beside her. LaRue closed the door to the corridor.

"Let me tell you our problem. Two women from this house have died in the last two weeks. Your discovery of the brass wedge gave us the only concrete piece of evidence we have that Huldah was struck, with intent to kill. Huldah Swenson was murdered, Mrs. Holliman."

"I know," Nan murmured.

"Good. Mrs. Devens died with a similar lack of concrete evidence as to how she died. For reasons of—er—policy, we have let it be known that this was her second—and successful—attempt at suicide. We have also said the black bag was not found. It was. In the well, also. With the exception of two Hindu mottoes and a small volume of very elementary exercises—spiritual exercises—that bag contains only personal clothing and toilet articles, the sort of thing any woman might pack. Perhaps she packed that bag: perhaps she didn't. But Mrs. Devens did not go down that well of her own accord. She was dead, had been for some hours, before she entered the water."

He paused, his eyes following the changing expressions on her face.

"You mean—she didn't kill—try to kill Huldah? That someone else—killed them both?"

"I didn't say that, but it's possible. There is a similarity in the—the techniques of these two deaths that suggests the same brain and hand are responsible."

"Then I can't help you," Nan declared, relieved. "I know the same things my husband knows—only not so much."

"Let me be the judge of that. Suppose you go back to the day you arrived here. Think of anything that struck you as odd. Take your time. Don't try to remember significant things. Just small things. That didn't match up with what you've heard or seen or thought."

"Oh. The first thing of course was an odd, dreadful sound—"

"Yes. I know about that. And Thor gave us the explanation. The old madrona was the culprit. It had many dead and rotted branches. After periods of heavy rain or fog or snow, moisture draining down and out some rotten spot produced that sound. It was so soft it couldn't be heard for more than a few feet, and then only on still days."

Mr. Ramsey inched his chair closer. "That's something you and your husband both know. What I want you to give me is observations of your own—too unimportant perhaps for you to have thought worth mentioning."

Nan lay back on her pillows, following herself through the days. "Well, I thought it odd that Beulah spent so much time in the kitchen. She's always cooking, or doing something there. But from the windows she can see the road, watch all the doors. Is that what you mean?"

"Splendid. Go on. Why?"

"I thought it was so she could watch Fleur. Fleur hasn't left this house since we came, except once, to go in to Seattle for Huldah's service. And Peggy went with her. And Peggy and Beulah came back with her. Eileen watched her, too. Peggy, not so much." Nan smiled faintly. "She watches Thor."

Mr. Ramsey smiled, too, nodded. "Anything else?"

"Well, that Fleur always wears black—though she has no reason to, now. Her grandfather's been dead, three years—"

Dyke's hand on the footboard lifted in an odd, quick way. As she turned her eyes on him, he put the hand in a pocket, nodded for her to continue.

"One awfully small thing I remember, I don't know why," she confessed after a long silence. "I'm sure it doesn't mean anything. But the day we came Fleur told us David adored to play with colored wooden beads. Yet I've never seen them—in her room or the nursery or when she took him downstairs or in here to play. He always has stuffed animals, blocks, things like that."

She stopped.

"What struck you as odd about that, Mrs. Holliman?" Jud LaRue prompted.

"I—I thought at first she had put them away because—they had frightened David. She said—he had almost choked her with a string she made for him. But later she said Mrs. Devens did that—made those bruises. I don't know, really, why I thought it odd not to see beads anywhere."

She was silent, feeling a bit foolish for revealing that her mind could be engaged by anything so trivial. Mr. Ramsey watched her for a moment, then stood up. "Thank you, Mrs. Holliman. You're tired, and I won't press you further now. But that's the sort of thing I'm looking for. If you think of anything else—"

He returned briskly to the sitting room for his brief case, coat, and hat. Jud followed him in, a moment later called Dyke.

Nan listened to the rumble of their voices, but no words came to her. After a time the district attorney and Jud went away. Dyke came back to her.

"How's that arm, hon? Think we could carry you downstairs tonight? I'd like to throw a party in the living room for everyone, including David. And you're to be guest of honor."

"Dyke! Does that mean—they aren't coming back? That everything's over!"

"Could be," he said.

34
Sunday Evening, January 27

The party was in full swing when the sheriff arrived. Nan lay in state on the couch, straws bent so she could drink orange juice while the others had highballs. All but David. He had orange juice too as he lay on the rug before the fire, straws bent so that he might drink as Nan did. Every other minute he had to sit up to make sure he was duplicating Nan's motions exactly.

For the first time laughter, free laughter, sounded in the old house.

"Hi, folks," Jud greeted them from the archway. "No one answered my knock on the back door, so I came right in."

"Hi!" Thor said, rising. "Come in and drink the health of our armless wonder. A broken head and a sprained arm, and she insists she's all right. Say when."

The sheriff shook his head, and the smile he had forced to his lips faded. "No," he said with difficulty. "I was just passing by—on my way home. Remembered I'd found something today David might like."

He sat down in the chair facing the fire Dyke had placed for him, began to pat his pockets. Fleur lifted David to his feet, pulled down his fuzzy blue bathrobe.

"Jud has a present for you, darling. Go see what it is."

David looked around, hesitated. Then, with the flattering attention of everyone on him, moved forward boldly.

When he was halfway across the floor, Jud pulled his hand put of his pocket, held out a bright string of wooden beads—red, blue, green, yellow, purple.

David stopped, his blue eyes growing wide. "Mine! Foo, mine!"

"Of course they're yours, sonny," Jud assured him. "Come and get them."

He held out his hand steadily. His lips still smiled, but his eyes were shining like hard blue porcelain.

Fleur was on her feet, her body tensed, looking at the beads also. The others sat motionless, their laughter stilled.

Thor rose, too. Uncertainly he looked from Jud to David, then to Fleur.

Feeling the tension and the attention too, David stamped a flannel foot angrily. "Bad!" he shrieked. "Bad-bad-bad!" Then he started for the beads.

He never reached them. Fleur flew at him, thrust him aside. She snatched the beads from Jud's outstretched hand and, whirling in one motion, hurled them into the fire.

She turned then on the sheriff. "How dare you! How dare you!"

He rose awkwardly to his feet, took a step toward her. "That was just a string of beads—from a dime store, Miss Fleur. No reason David couldn't have *them.*"

She shrank back from him, her hands flying to her throat. The angry color drained from her face. Her eyes dilated as she gazed at him.

The sheriff stood motionless, his own eyes never leaving hers.

She moved her lips, but no sound came from them. They seemed parched, and she touched them swiftly with her tongue. "You know! You know!"

"Yes, I know, Miss Fleur. Beads like those choked Mrs. Devens to death. Were flung into the well with the bag—"

Fleur swayed, then steadied as Thor moved toward her. "No! No! Keep away from me! All of you!"

Her arms went out, motioning him and Dyke back. Her eyes remained on the sheriff. "What are you going to do?"

"Arrest you for the murder of Mrs. Ruby Devens."

Her head snapped back as if under a blow. Dyke moved forward. But Fleur needed no support from him. From anyone. Slowly she regained control of her body and voice. Stood erect, relaxed.

"I'm glad, Jud. I'll be glad when it's over."

"Fleur," Dyke warned quickly, "don't say anything. You don't need to—"

She turned to look at him, to look at each of the strained, sealed faces watching her. Last of all she looked at Thor, then David, drooping now against Thor's shoulder.

"He should be in bed now, Thor." She looked round, found Peggy, standing in shadow, pressed back against the wall in the shelter of the outjutting fireplace. "Go with them, Peg. Take good care of them—both."

Thor shook his head, turned to place David in Peg's arms.

"No." Fleur's soft voice held finality. "This is good-by, Thor. I shan't see you again. I don't want to see you—any of you again. I know what I'm doing. Please go."

She would say no more, standing inflexibly beside Jud until first Peg, then Thor with David, vanished beyond the curtains. For a moment she listened, head bent, to their hushed steps on the stairs.

Then she turned to Dyke. "I'm glad you're here. You know Grandfather Wales' plan for Madrona Place. You can carry it out—for the others. I'll give you my power of attorney to handle my share—for Thor and David. With one change. This house and three acres were to remain as my home. Thor can do as he likes with the land. *But destroy this house*. Tear it down. No one must live in it again. David must not grow up here."

"Fleur," Dyke advised again, "don't talk now. There'll be plenty of time—later."

"No. This is the last time I'll see any of you. I shan't be sorry." Scorn glittered in her eyes as they touched Beulah, then Eileen. "Promise about the house, Dyke?"

"But Thor must be consulted—"

"Madrona Place is not his—yet. It is mine."

When Dyke remained silent, she cried, "David must not live in this house! Must I tell you why? Because it's full of hate and fear and greed and death! Not peaceful death—murder!"

"Miss Fleur," Jud LaRue put out a quieting hand, "come with me now. You're—"

"Don't touch me. I'll go with you. But first I must make sure David will not live here."

"Nonsense!" Beulah's voice was harsh. "You've lost all right to dictate, Fleur."

Fleur's glance silenced her. It was soft, luminous, but under it Beulah sat back, her hands gripping the arms of her chair.

"I've bought that right—with my life," Fleur said steadily. "Grandfather Wales thought to take Madrona Place from me—when he discovered I'd married Thor. He died—before he could change his will."

"Miss Fleur!" Even Jud LaRue's eyes were expressive now. "You don't know what you're saying."

"I gave him his medicine. The day he accused me of carrying Thor's child—he wouldn't believe we were married—I—stopped giving it to him."

"That can't be true, Fleur," Nan cried. "Huldah—"

"Huldah knew!" In the speechless silence Fleur rushed on, concern for David unleashing her long-sealed tongue.

"She knew. And she said nothing. Because she wanted David. And Madrona Place—all of it—for David. So did I—and under the will I controlled the money. She got him away from me when he was born, but last spring she brought him back. But she was afraid of me then. For herself. Then Ruby and Beulah, Eileen, Peggy came. She was afraid of them, too. For David."

"But it was Huldah who sent for them," Dyke reminded her. "You told the district attorney that yourself."

"She did. Thinking to find in them a weapon against me. But when each one came, she saw them for what they were. Greedy only for what they could get out of Madrona Place themselves—right now. She'd kept all Grandfather's accounts, handled all his correspondence—first to keep Madrona Place for me. Then, when David was born, for him. She destroyed all the correspondence, hid the records in the madrona before she came to the hospital in Idaho where I was, to take David. She held them and Grandfather's death over my head to have him for herself. But I knew she'd never use them. By one, she'd lose most of Madrona Place for David. By the other, blacken the Wales name—and his future."

"Why did she send for me?" Dyke asked then.

"You were her last resort. She planned to tell you, give you the records. And she tried to steal David away—to take him to you. I caught her with him in her arms. Then she tried to slip away herself—"

A ripple of horror went round the room. Jud raised a hand again to silence her. But she drew back from him, rushed on.

"I saw her go down the back stairs. I had to stop her. I ran down the front stairs, took that desk piece—with a crazy idea of making her think it was a gun—in the dark. And followed her. . . ."

"Mrs. Devens saw you?" Jud asked then.

"She saw everything, spied on every move I made. She heard Huldah in my room, listened at the door to what we said. Then she saw me go down the stairs. She followed me."

"You saw her?"

"No. But I knew she knew. She was so terrified—and I was terrified of her. That she'd betray me. Eileen is so clever, watching, saying nothing, waiting."

Beulah made a choked sound, managed, "Ruby didn't try to kill herself—"

"No. I gave her that whisky and veronal. But your ears are always alert, aren't they, Beulah? I heard you go down the corridor for Dyke. That was when I made my one mistake. I should have stayed, made Ruby drink it. There was time. Instead, I slipped across to my room. Later—when Ruby was asleep and you'd left her—I went back. With David's wooden beads. He'd almost choked me with them. I knew how—"

"Fleur!" Beulah's black eyes turned glassy. "Ruby wasn't sleeping—Wednesday morning—when I saw her!"

"She was asleep—forever." Fleur turned from her to Jud. "When Beulah and Eileen had gone into Seattle and Peggy was in the garage, I carried Ruby down the back stairs—out to the well. She wasn't heavy," she added irrelevantly. "She just looked that way—with all those sweaters and skirts."

"The bag," Jud said.

"That was already packed, ready. I took that, too. And the beads. That night the storm began? I thought I was safe. I was safe—until I saw Nan looking down into the well. She came into the house so quickly, I was afraid—"

"*You pushed Nan!*" Dyke accused, incredulous.

"I pushed Nan," she told him calmly. "I tried to kill her, too. Perhaps if I had told you only that, it would have been enough. Now will you do as I say about this house?

I killed three people, tried to kill a fourth—for David. I
wanted him to have Madrona Place—all of it."

Tenaciously she faced Dyke. "Well?"

"You win," he agreed bleakly. "This house comes down
if I have to wreck it myself."

Fleur turned back to Jud LaRue. "I'm ready."

The sheriff moved like a man in a dream. He seemed
unable to credit this thing he had done himself—with a
string of beads.

"You can—you'll need some things, won't you, Miss
Fleur? You can take a bag."

She shook her head. "I brought nothing with me when
I came to this house. I'll take nothing out of it."

While he still gazed at her, she moved ahead of him
to the archway, turned there to look once more about the
long room. She was a striking figure in black and white
against the dull green. Her black hair and black eyes shining, the long black gown modeled about her slender body;
only her oval face and long hands white.

Watching her, Nan's eyes filled. Fleur's life had been
like that, she thought. Black. And white. No grays. No
compromises. "Morning becomes Electra," Dyke murmured to Eileen, beside him. "I only understood that yesterday. But you've known from the first?"

"What value, knowing? I could find no proof."

Fleur heard. "No, you couldn't, could you?" she said
contemptuously. "For all your watching and prying. Any
of you. Because you were all cowards. Because you wanted
Madrona Place without cost to yourselves or your name!
Do you think I didn't know you knew? I knew—and I
knew your tricks, too. You brought David down that night;
thinking to frighten me, didn't you? You failed. I saw you
take that key from my pocket yourself. . . .

"Peggy tried to frighten me too. With a scarf of Ruby's
on my pillow! It served its purpose—concealed my hand

in the darkness when Nan opened that back-stairs door. I dropped it on the floor in Thor's room. He disposed of it nicely—for me."

Her eyes came back scornfully to Dyke. "And you— with a bit of glass, you tried to trap me, too!" Her hand motioned slightly to the fire. "There is your trap—"

He ignored that to ask incredulously, "Are you saying Thor knew—helped you?"

"Thor?" Her expression changed, grew sad. "No. Poor boy. Huldah had impressed him too thoroughly that a Wales could do no wrong. The only non-Wales was Ruby. He blamed her for everything. Her incense burning and mumbo-jumbo to his good Lutheran soul meant only one thing—that she was in league with the devil. He made me collect all her paraphernalia, while he searched her stuff in the barn and garage. Then at midnight Thursday we burned everything in the apple house."

She smiled faintly. *"He* swore *me* to secrecy! Poor boy. He tried so hard to take care of me—to be all I wanted. And I wanted only Madrona Place. And David."

That name roused her from the half-reverie in which she spoke.

"David!" she repeated softly. "My own son—with his love for bright beads—"

She turned to Jud LaRue. "You alone understood that only David could—could betray me."

Quickly she thrust open the curtains, stepped into the foyer. The sheriff, his heavy shoulders sagging, followed her.

About the Author

Vera Kelsey (1892-1961) was the daughter of an American couple, born in Winnipeg, Ontario. She grew up in Grand Forks, North Dakota. She was a reporter for the *Fargo Forum,* and graduated from the University of North Dakota. Her early writing career included working for the *North China Daily News,* which allowed her to travel extensively in Asia, and then she spent almost five years in South America, particularly Brazil, before making her home in New York. She wrote mystery novels, travel books, and historical and regional nonfiction. She spent her last years in Minneapolis, and owned a cottage on Lake Minnetonka.

THE OWL
SANG
THREE
TIMES

VERA KELSEY

SATAN
HAS SIX
FINGERS

VERA KELSEY

Coachwhip
Publications

CoachwhipBooks.com

Coachwhip
Publications

WHISPER
MURDER!

VERA KELSEY

THE BRIDE
DINED
ALONE

VERA KELSEY

CoachwhipBooks.com

Coachwhip
Publications

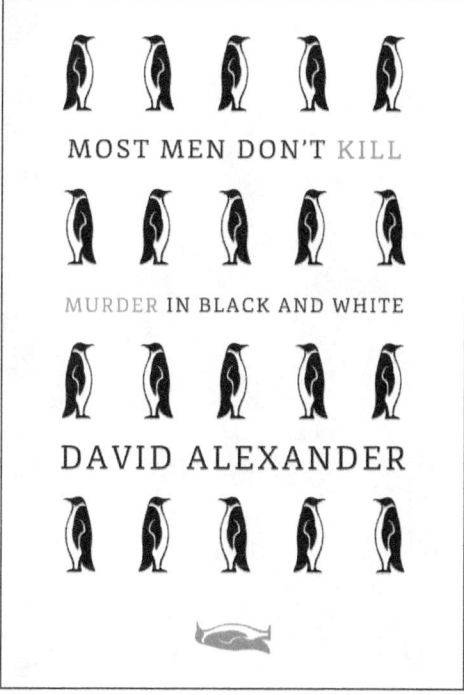

MOST MEN DON'T KILL

MURDER IN BLACK AND WHITE

DAVID ALEXANDER

CoachwhipBooks.com

MURDER AT DRAKE'S ANCHORAGE

E. LEE WADDELL

Coachwhip
Publications

DEATH
SERVES
AN ACE

HELEN WILLS
AND
JOHN W. MURPHY

CoachwhipBooks.com

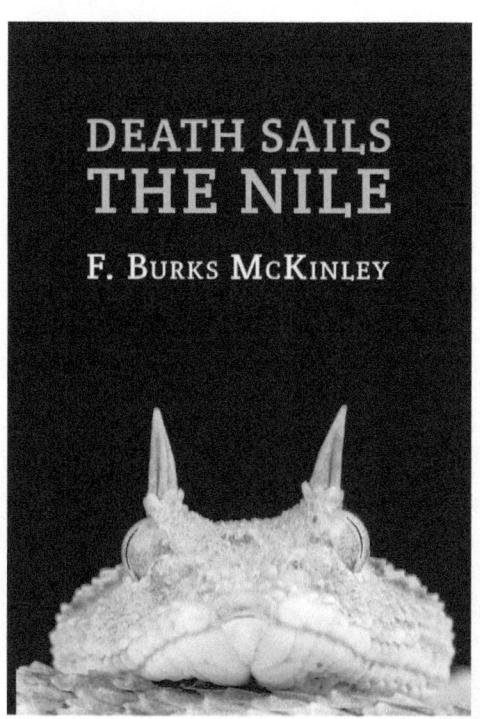

DEATH SAILS
THE NILE

F. Burks McKinley

Coachwhip
Publications

DESIGN
for MURDER

Frederic Arnold Kummer

CoachwhipBooks.com

Jack Dolph

MURDER
MAKES
THE MARE GO

Coachwhip
Publications

THE
RUMBLE
MURDERS

Henry Ware Eliot, Jr.

CoachwhipBooks.com

MURDER OF
THE HONEST BROKER

WILLOUGHBY SHARP

Coachwhip
Publications

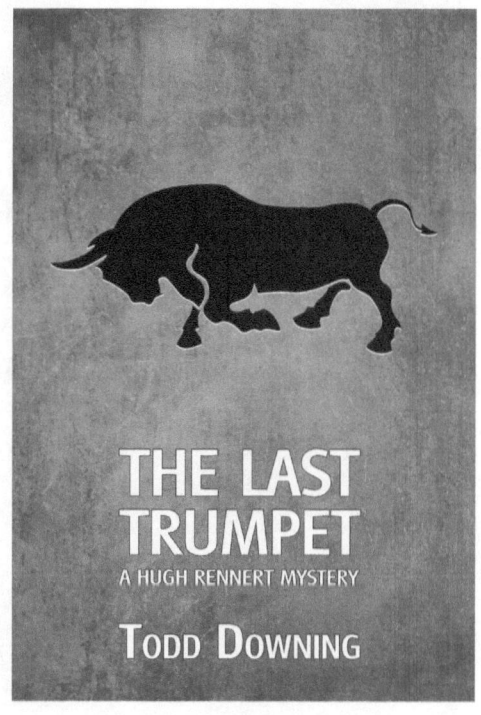

THE LAST
TRUMPET
A HUGH RENNERT MYSTERY

TODD DOWNING

CoachwhipBooks.com

Coachwhip
Publications

CoachwhipBooks.com

www.ingramcontent.com/pod-product-compliance
Lightning Source LLC
Chambersburg PA
CBHW020825260626
47169CB00003B/833